THREE'S A CHARM

MAGIC AND MAYHEM, BOOK SIX

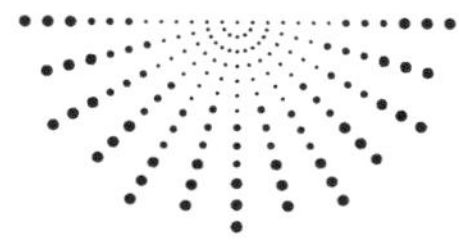

ROBYN PETERMAN

WWW.ROBYNPETERMAN.COM

Cover by *Rebecca Poole of dreams2media*
Edited by *Meg Weglarz*

❀ Created with Vellum

BOOKS IN THIS SERIES

Switching Hour

Witch Glitch

A Witch In Time

Magically Delicious

A Tale Of Two Witches

Three's A Charm

WHAT OTHERS ARE SAYING

"If Amy Schumer and Janet Evanovitch had a baby, it would be Robyn Peterman!"

~Dakota Cassidy

USA Today Best Selling Author

"Funny, fast-paced, and filled with laugh-out-loud dialogue. Robyn Peterman delivers a sidesplitting, sexy tale of powerful witches and magical delights. I devoured it in one sitting!"

~Ann Charles

USA Today Bestselling Author

of the *Deadwood Humorous Mystery Series*

ACKNOWLEDGMENTS

The Magic and Mayhem Series is a delight to write. However, writing the story is only part of the journey to getting the book published. There are many people to thank and I'm a lucky girl to have such a talented and wonderful support system.

Rebecca Poole—your covers are as brilliant as you are. Thank you.

Meg Weglarz—your editing always makes me look better than I am. Thank you.

Donna McDonald—a gal couldn't ask for a tougher, brilliant and more awesome critique partner. Thank you.

Wanda and Susan—you are the best-est beta readers in the world. Thank you.

Wanda—you rock hard. Thank you, thank you and thank you again.

My family—none of this would be worth it without you. Thank you for being mine. I adore you.

DEDICATION

For Stephanie.
You have brought my warped imagination to life.
I adore you.

CHAPTER ONE

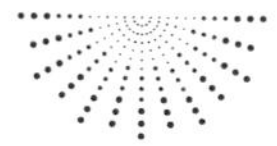

"Would you rather eat a vat of salad dressing or six rolls of toilet paper?" Sassy asked as she dusted off her broom in anticipation of our afternoon excursion.

"Can I soak the toilet paper in water first?"

Sassy tilted her head and considered the request. "Yes, that would be okay I suppose."

"What kind of salad dressing?" I inquired as I shoved my profane and socially unacceptable familiar off the sofa.

The obese furry butthole had been sharpening his claws on my leather couch. My choices were to declaw him, de-hair him or shove his enormous kitty butt off of it. I went for the kindest of the three. He landed with a thud and a string of swear words that made me grin.

"Miracle Whip," Sassy answered.

"That's mayonnaise."

"Noooo, Zelda. The jar says salad dressing. Jars don't lie," she informed me.

"Umm, okay… but when you say salad dressing, I think of French or Italian."

Sassy's massive eye roll alerted me that something appalling was about to leave her mouth. She rarely disappointed.

"Listen, little missy, we're playing 'Would You Rather'. I *asked* you if you would rather eat a vat of salad dressing or six rolls of toilet paper. I *did not* ask you if you wanted to eat a country. Countries are entirely too big to eat. Period."

"I *said* French or Italian," I repeated.

"I *heard* you," she shot back, waving the bushy end of her broom at me. "French and Italian are full of people and cars and shopping malls. It would be impossible to eat them. The game has to be real. You feel me?"

"Youse want me to gag her or blast her ass out da front door, Doll Face?" Fat Bastard asked, leg perched high over his head without even looking up from his morning nad cleanse.

I actually considered it for a brief moment and then sadly shook my head. While Sassy had come a long way, she was still sorely lacking in the brains department.

"Youse is losing your touch, Zelda," Fat Bastard pointed out as he took a quick break from his rank habit. "If youse ain't gonna zap her, youse gotta call her something rude."

"You're correct. Suggestions?"

"Lumpy Bulge Spasm gots a nice ring to it," Fat Bastard announced and then went back to his slurpy routine.

"That's almost as disgusting as you are," I told him, trying not to laugh.

"Thanks, Sweet Cheeks. I got tons of 'em—Trashy Weiner Buccaneer, Crusty Turd Juggler, Rusty Ass Pixie…"

"Stop," I shouted. "I'm gonna have to go back to my idiot therapist, Roger the rabbit, to get my brain wiped if you keep that shit up."

"One more?" Fat Bastard pleaded with an evil little smirk on his kitty face.

"No."

"Please?"

"No."

"Steamy Ass Demon," he grunted and then hauled ass out of the room at warp speed—amazing for an animal as rotund as he was.

"Your cat is a Dumbass Dong Gremlin," Sassy said, grinning from ear to ear.

"I'd have to go for Ball Licking Foul-Mouthed Douche Canoe," I replied.

Sassy's laugh bounced through the room and I giggled. She drove me all kinds of crazy, but she was loyal to a fault even if she did pilfer my belongings every now and then.

Our introduction to each other had been under less than auspicious circumstances. We'd both been doing time in the magical big house for misuse of our power among other infractions. I swore to the Goddess that once I got sprung from the pokey I would avoid her like the plague. However, the grand plan of life didn't exactly work out that way.

Nope, here I was in Assjacket, West Virginia happier than I'd ever been in my entire life—a fact that gave me nightmares occasionally. I had Mac, my mate—the most gorgeous werewolf on the planet and we had two perfectly beautiful twin babies, Audrey and Henry. I was terrified I'd blow out puppies due to the fact that I was in a cross-species relationship, but thank the Goddess I didn't. All of the violent threats I'd made to Mac's man bits were for naught—which is a good thing. I loved his man bits.

My job as the Shifter Whisperer, or Shifter Wanker as I preferred, kept me busy because Shifters were extremely fucking accident-prone. I complained constantly so my reputation as an uncaring, materialistic witch stayed secure, but sadly it was being systematically shredded. Everyone thought I was nice and good and kind. It was freakin' horrible.

Glancing down at her phone, Sassy gasped and then laughed. "Zelda, we have a problem."

"Don't you mean, Houston?" I shot back with a grin.

She stared at me blankly and then narrowed her eyes.

"When did you change your name to *Houston* and why didn't I know about it?" Sassy demanded.

I sighed and sat on my hands so I didn't zap her bald. "I didn't. I was referring to *Apollo 13*."

"I just learned French," Sassy hissed. "I do not know Chinese. If you don't speak English, I'm gonna have to wax you."

With a flick of my fingers, I duct taped her mouth shut. The old me would have given her a massive wart in the middle of her face and turned her hair green. Goddess in gaucho pants, I *was* losing my touch. Fat Bastard was correct and it made me itchy.

Deciding to make her bowlegged if she rode my nerves even an inch farther, I removed the tape—with my hands. It was far more dramatic.

"Motherhumper on a unicycle," Sassy grunted. "I was joking. I wouldn't wax you. If I did, I'd live in fear the rest of my life waiting for your retribution."

"You just spoke Chinese," I pointed out.

"I did?" she asked, confused but clearly impressed with herself.

"Yep. Now what's the problem?"

She handed me her phone and I scanned the text quickly. What the ever-loving hell?

"No," I said. "I'm not healing that."

"Don't you have to?" she asked, wincing as she reread the text over my shoulder.

"I fix wounds. I don't heal stupidity. I'm not a miracle worker. I'm a witch," I snapped. "Plus I have to take on the pain of the dumbasses when I heal them. I have no intention of taking that on."

"Don't you mean patient?

"Same thing."

"Right," Sassy said, with a nod of understanding. "That's why you gave me a frozen bag of veggies after the tragedy of my Brazilian."

Rolling my head to relieve tension and the desire to blow both Sassy and Assjacket off the face of the planet, I nodded. I didn't trust anything nice to leave my lips, so I opted for silent communication. My maturity appalled me.

"Do you think it will heal on its own?" she asked, trying not to laugh.

"Don't know. Don't care. I didn't sign up for shit like this."

"Did you actually sign up at all?"

"No," I shouted. "I did not sign up for this. I was blackmailed into it by Baba Yobuttinski, our fashion disaster of a boss."

"Not to mention your dad's girlfriend," Sassy reminded me as if I needed a reminder.

"Do you hate me?" I asked with fingers twitching to give her a permanent Mohawk. However, the fact that my dad was dating the worst dressed and bossiest witch in existence wasn't Sassy's fault. At all.

"Umm… no."

"Just checking," I replied. "Because only mortal enemies who want to be bald would mention the gag-inducing fact that my Fabdudio is shagging Baba Yostuckintheeighties."

"My bad," Sassy said quickly while checking to make sure she still had hair. "Won't mention it again."

We both sat in silence after my outburst and stared at the offending text.

"He seems pretty desperate," Sassy pointed out. "He even offered to send a picture."

My gag reflex kicked in and I wiggled my fingers, blowing Sassy's phone into oblivion. Goddess that felt good. "Well, now he can't. Problem solved."

"That was my phone," Sassy said.

"Yep," I said as my hair began to blow wildly around my head and my body began to glow. "Your point?"

"Umm, no point," she said, backing away and getting under my coffee table.

"Grab your broom," I instructed as I conjured up a broom for myself.

We didn't need brooms to fly, but Sassy loved riding hers so I thought I'd give it a try. I knew we'd look like idiots zooming through the air on cleaning apparatuses, but I figured it would alarm the dumbass we were going to visit. We didn't need wands or any of the other witchy crap from fairy tales. The Goddess blessed us with our magic and it came from within.

"You're gonna ride a broom?" Sassy asked, delighted.

"I'm gonna ride a broom," I confirmed. "It's all about the entrance and we're going to make a memorable one."

"Where are we going?"

"We're going to pay Roger, the horny, jackhole, porn-loving, idiot rabbit a visit."

"Holy shit," she gasped out, trying not to laugh. "For real?"

"Yep, let me just leave Mac a quick note. He took Henry and Audrey to our secret garden. He thinks they might shift soon and doesn't want them to tear the house up."

"I thought they didn't shift till they were older."

"They're… unique," I said with a grin and a shake of my head. "My babies are one… I mean, two of a kind."

And that was an understatement. The Goddess had gifted my children with powers I couldn't yet comprehend. I was still working on my mom skills since I'd had the world's suckiest maternal parental unit. At least I'd found my dad, even though I'd accidentally run him over with my car when we first met—hence my stay in the pokey.

Anyhoo, if their wet kisses and constant smiles were anything to go by, my kids loved me. And Goddess knew I loved them. I loved them with every fiber of my being.

However, I didn't love Roger the rabbit at this moment in time. And he was about to catch wind of that little fact.

CHAPTER TWO

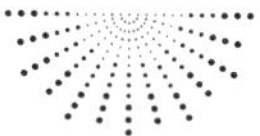

Riding a broom sucked ass.

It was uncomfortable and hard to stay upright on it. I'd flown upside down for a good fifteen minutes of our trip, much to Sassy's delight. She'd laughed so hard I'd had no choice but to turn half of her blonde hair blue. It was the least evil thing I could think of with all the blood in my body residing in my brain due to my being head down and legs in the air. Thank the Goddess I wasn't going commando today.

"Will this wash out?" Sassy asked, pulling on her curls as we approached the town.

"Nope," I replied, scanning the crowd below and gripping the broom so hard I was sure it would crack in half. I was just hoping for a landing that didn't give me a concussion.

Our town, if you could call it that, consisted of Main Street. The town square was dominated by a cement statue of a bear missing one side of his head. The rest of the block included a barbershop, hardware store, gas station, diner, a few other rundown buildings, and a mom and pop grocery store.

It was a total dump and that suited the Shifters of Assjacket just fine. Humans drove right through the dilapidated town without a backward glance. Inside the ramshackle structures, everything was pure enchantment. Everything from the Assjacket Diner to my idiot therapist Roger the rabbit's office was charming and lovely behind the broken down exteriors. The town was a massive sleight of hand, so to speak. It was a testament to the brilliance of my friends since the Shifters and witches lived very public yet secret lives.

The square was packed. Apparently, all of Assjacket was concerned about Roger's *problem* and had turned up for the show… or showdown to be more accurate.

"Incoming," Sassy shrieked as we swooped into the crowd of Shifters staring in horror at Roger's malady.

"Motherfucker in a tutu," I grunted as I slammed into the backside of my dear friend Simon the skunk and sent him flying into the cement bear. The gasps from the crowd at my horrifying arrival weren't quite the reaction I was going for, but at least I hadn't killed myself or anyone else. I called it a win.

"Simon, you okay?" I asked as I flicked my fingers and burned my broom to a crisp. I was never riding that stupid stick again.

"I'm good," he said, jogging over and giving me a hug. "A little surprised, but fine."

Heaving out a sigh of relief, I hugged him back. He'd been one of my first friends when I'd arrived in Assjacket and I adored him. I'd feel awful if I'd damaged him—not to mention he tended to blow off stinkers when he was alarmed.

Air was clear. Simon was fine. Broom was incinerated. However, there was still an *issue*.

"It's bad," Wanda the raccoon Shifter whispered, trying with all her might not to grin.

Wanda, another of my besties, was the owner of the Assjacket Diner, along with DeeDee the deer. She was no bullshit and baked the best cheesecakes in the Goddess's Universe. If Wanda said it was bad… It was bad.

Roger was going to be lucky to live at this point.

The idiot in question was my therapist. He was a porno-addicted rabbit Shifter with a fabulous reputation as a head shrinker. I had to admit—albeit privately and to no living being—he was good at his job. He'd helped me get out of my own way and realize I was a lovable witch, but he was still a dumbass of epic proportions.

The rabbit of the hour was sitting on a cushioned lawn chair in the middle of Main Street with a blanket draped over his bottom half. My asschiatrist was holding court and laughing with the good folk of Assjacket. However, he *was* a bit pale.

"How did this happen?" I asked Wanda as I made my way toward Roger.

"He humped a log," she replied and then fell to her knees in hysterics.

I froze. I was torn between joining Wanda on the ground or zapping Roger straight to hell.

"Repeat," I said, praying to the Goddess I'd heard her wrong.

Wanda was useless. She was laughing so hard, she was crying. Whatever. I'd get to the bottom of this with or without any intel.

As I approached, the crowd parted and Roger had the decency to blush.

"I was hoping you'd come," he said, giving me a weak wave and a chuckle.

"You want to explain?" I asked, slapping my hands on my hips and giving him the evil eye.

"Umm… no?" he suggested.

"Umm… yes," I shot back as my fingers began to spark and my wild red hair began to blow around my head.

The Shifters were smart. Within seconds of beginning my little chat with Roger, they'd all run for cover. However, Sassy stayed right at my side. For as annoying as she could be, she always had my back. Not that her having my back was always a good thing, but it was a thing, and I loved her for it.

"Shall I just show you?" he suggested.

"Will I have to bathe my eyes in bleach if you do?" I inquired.

"Yes," Bob the unibrowed beaver shouted from beneath a bush in front of the grocery.

"Who did I screw over in a former life to have to deal with this shit?" I muttered as I paced back and forth and tried to decide what to do.

I was a healer witch and part of my job was to heal the Shifters of Assjacket along with keeping the magical balance in my area. But this was clearly not an accidental injury.

"You humped a log?" I questioned through gritted teeth as Sassy started to laugh.

"I didn't actually *intentionally* hump it, per se," Roger explained.

"So you *accidentally* humped the unsuspecting log?"

"It sounds so sordid when you put it that way," he protested.

"Umm… how else should I put it?" I snapped. "Did the log jump out and hump you?"

Roger's little head dropped to his chest and his nose began to twitch making him look like a human rabbit—a sad and embarrassed human rabbit. Now I felt bad. Damn it. Why should I feel bad that he humped a log and injured his joystick?

"You want me to look?" Sassy volunteered.

"You would do that for me?" I asked, shocked, impressed and grossed out.

"Yes," she said. "I love you. You're my best friend and you have the worst gag reflex of anyone I know."

And now I felt awful. I'd just turned the hair blue of the person who was willing to assess the wanker damage of my shit for brains therapist. If that wasn't true friendship, I didn't know what was. With a wiggle of my nose, I turned Sassy's luxurious locks back to their beautiful blonde glory.

"We'll look together," I said, taking her hand in mine.

"You sure?" she asked.

"No."

"Okay, let's do it," Sassy whispered, pulling me forward with effort. "Should we take a picture? You know, for future blackmail purposes," she suggested, yanking hard on my hand.

"Already done," Bob shouted from his bush.

Jerking Sassy to a halt, I turned towards Bob's voice. I was *not* happy that I was about to see the package of my therapist, but I really didn't like that Unibrow Bob had taken a picture of Roger's humiliating *accident*. I wasn't nice, but I also wasn't a dick—absolutely no pun intended.

"Give me your phone, Bob," I hissed with my hands raised ready to blast his ass sky high if he refused.

"It's new," he protested.

"And your point?" I asked, snapping my fingers and elevating him about twenty feet in the air.

"No point, Zelda," he choked out and tossed me his phone.

I promptly crushed in under my fabulous Doc Martens hot pick combat boots and then let Bob drop to the ground with a thud.

"Hear me now, people," I shouted to the hiding townsfolk of my adopted city. "Clearly Roger and his peen have had an altercation with a log. This is unfortunate on many levels and Roger may not live to hump another day. But no one—and I mean *no one*—will bully anyone or take unflattering photos of other's stupidity especially when it involves weenies. Am I clear?"

A shamed chorus of yesses came from under buildings, trees and bushes.

And then I saw it.

Goddess, help me.

It wasn't pretty and I had no intention in this lifetime of touching it. Yes, it was my job as Shifter Wanker to heal my people, but *this*... This didn't count. And if it did, I was going to quit.

Not only would touching the painful looking wee-wee break some kind of patient slash therapist law, it would induce nightmares for the rest of my unnaturally long life. Not to mention whatever body part I healed on a Shifter or witch, I took the pain into my own body. Seeing as how I didn't exactly have a man tool, I was unsure how I'd come out of this shit show.

"I can't do this," I muttered as Sassy went over to a tree, broke off a branch and handed it to me.

"Use this," she said.

"For what?"

"To poke it and fix it," Sassy suggested with a wince and a gag. "I mean, as a white witch, your Earth energy should be able to go through the stick and you can fix that pecker right up. That way you don't actually have to handle the trouser snake."

"John Holmes," Bob's disembodied voice called out from the shrub he was hiding under.

"Excuse me?" I snapped, pointing the stick at Bob's bush.

"Roger named his member John Holmes. It might be less confusing just to call his salami by its given name," Bob suggested.

I vaguely recalled a group package-naming debacle from a year ago, but I'd blocked it out. Of course Bob, in his infinite lack of wisdom and concern for my gag reflex, had to go and remind me. I was glad I'd smashed his phone. If he volunteered another piece of unsavory information he was going to pay.

"Umm… Bob?" I said so calmly I heard the entire population of Assjacket gasp in terror.

"Yes?" he squeaked out.

"If you feel the need to say anything else, I'd suggest you keep it to yourself. Because if you speak I will lower your hairline to your upper lip. This will be permanent, wildly unattractive and I will let everyone take pictures. You feel me?"

Bob's grunt of understanding didn't count as words, so I let it go.

"I'm not calling your pickle John Holmes," I told Roger.

"That's fine," he assured me. "He answers to anything."

Closing my eyes, I counted to twenty-five and a half. This had been such a promising day. Now? Not so much. It took everything

I had not to wiggle my fingers and remove Roger's friend completely.

"Here's the deal. I'm going to wing this one and use a spell. I can't touch it. I still need about twenty-two and three quarters more years of therapy and if I handle your wang, that disqualifies you," I told him.

Roger nodded in understanding. "I see your point."

"Plus I don't think Mac would be delighted that I poked your wonder worm even with a stick," I added.

My man was the King of this ragtag group of Shifters and wildly powerful. He was also a little possessive. Actually I was equally as possessive, so we basically canceled each other out. It worked out great and the sex was off the charts.

"I agree," Roger said. "And by the by, I'm sorry."

Sighing, I smiled at the rabbit who had helped me beyond words. It was the least I could do to make his *issue* better. However, touching it was still out of the question.

And if he ever pulled this shit again, he was on his own.

"It's okay… kind of," I said. "I just hope you learned your lesson."

"What lesson?" Sassy asked.

"Humping logs is a no-no," I said, shaking my head in defeat. Never in a million years did I think that sentence would come out of my mouth.

"Got it," she said. "I'll let everyone know."

"You do that," I told her with a laugh.

"Do you still want to change your name to Houston? Now's a good time to do it since everyone in town is here," Sassy suggested.

"Umm… no. But thanks."

"No worries."

"All right Roger, you ready?" I asked, rolling my neck and cracking my knuckles in preparation for pulling a whopper of a spell out of my ass.

"Will this be painful?" he asked, paling considerably.

"Does the Pope sing karaoke every third Tuesday?" I asked.

"I have no idea," Roger replied with a wrinkled brow.

"And there's your answer. I have no motherhumpin' idea either," I told him truthfully.

"If I had to guess, I'd say there's a fifty-fifty chance it will hurt, a forty-seventy chance it will be painless, and a thirty-ninety chance you'll be a eunuch," Sassy told him.

"You just spoke Chinese again," I told Sassy.

"I did?" she squealed and danced around the empty street.

"Yes, you did. Now, I'd suggest you take cover. I've never done this and it could get messy."

Roger began to hyperventilate, but Sassy didn't move.

"I'm staying right here. If you go down in a blaze of exploding, projectile doinker, I'm going down with you," she said.

"Seriously?" I asked, unsure if I wanted to laugh or gag at her colorful description of what might happen.

"No, but I'm still staying."

Sassy's loyalty—or utter stupidity—humbled me. Note to self—stop turning Sassy's hair different colors and let her borrow my Birkin bag. It was the least I could do considering she was putting her life in possible harms way of being hit by a projectile penis.

"Roger, are you ever going to hump a log again?" I asked, narrowing my eyes at him.

"No. No, I will never hump a log again."

"Good."

"Do we need the log for the spell?" Sassy asked.

I paused for a brief second in thought and then gagged. "Umm… no. We do *not* need the log. I don't ever want to see that log. In fact I think someone should get rid of the log. Forever," I said, trying not to picture anything that would stick in my frontal lobe.

"I'm on it," Bob the beaver grunted as he crawled out from under the bush and jogged off into the woods.

The fact that Bob clearly knew where the log was disturbed me, but I pushed that to a part of my mind that I never visited.

"Okay, Roger. Try to relax. We'll have that pocket rocket patched up in a jiffy."

With a quick, silent and very heartfelt prayer to the Goddess, I pulled on my magic and let her rip...

Goddess on High, hear my plea
Roger the dumbass had a mishap with his... umm... rabbit wee-wee.
I know it is rare,
To use enchantment to repair.
But since I don't own a schlong,
I figured the regular way could go wrong.
Goddess, bless me with your magic,
And make Roger's thingie not so tragic.
Please, please, fucking please hear my call,
Cause I'll tell you this much—I'm not touching that freakin' weiner
—at all.

"So mote it be!" Sassy yelled as the wind whipped up and I felt an unusual tingling flash through my body.

Black sparks and fire left my fingertips, which was not the best of signs. It shocked me to the core since I thought I was using white magic for the spell. I was still trying to control the unwelcome dark magic in my body that I'd gotten thanks to my mother. However, I'd never healed with a spell. I'd always healed with touch. Dizziness washed over me and I felt ill. Quickly squatting so I didn't fall over, I prayed to the Goddess once again.

Roger's little body stiffened and he fell off the chair with a gasp and a shriek. My eyes went wide and my stomach plummeted. I hoped to the Next Adventure and back that I hadn't offed my therapist. He was a royal pain in my ass, but I secretly adored him. Killing him would so suck.

I felt rooted to the ground as Sassy dashed over to see what I'd done to Roger. "He's alive," she shouted triumphantly as she looked under the blanket.

"And?" I asked.

"And… well, it's definitely different from when we started."

"How different?" I whispered.

"*Five times* different," she said with eyes as round as saucers.

And that's when I passed out.

Clearly spells don't quite work for healing.

Shit.

CHAPTER THREE

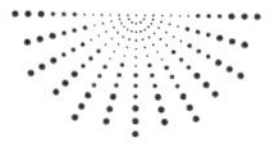

"Houston, are you okay?" I heard my father say in a desperately worried tone. Who in the Goddess's name was he talking to?

"Her pulse is fine and her breathing is normal," Baba Yaga said, touching my forehead with her cool hand. "She'll come to momentarily."

"Was it Houston's spell or the realization that Roger now has five wanks that made her faint?" Sassy asked in a hushed tone.

"Dat's a lotta licking dat rabbit is gonna have to do," Fat Bastard pointed out as my other furry familiars, Boba Fett and Jango Fett, grunted in impressed agreement.

Oh my hell, this had to be a dream. Right?

"This is not okay," Mac growled as he adjusted the pillow under my head. "Zelda doesn't need…"

"You mean Houston," Sassy corrected my mate.

Mac's sigh was long and I could feel his frustration even though my eyes wouldn't cooperate with me and open. "You're certain Zelda wants to change her name?"

"Positive," Sassy replied. "She called herself Houston like twelve times—or a least once—and came close to announcing it to the entire town before she turned Roger into a porno star for a freak show."

Damn it—not a dream.

"Accident," I croaked out, forcing my eyes open and trying to sit up.

It was strange that I'd passed out. I'd felt no pain when I'd used the spell to heal… or rather *enhance* Roger. Normally when I healed someone, it took me an hour or two to feel okay again. Of course the first time I healed my friends, I was out for a week, but that was a long time ago. I was a pro now.

Or maybe not.

"Oh my Goddess, Houston. I was so worried about you," Fabio, my dad, cried out as he took me in his arms and rocked me like a baby.

My dad was still making up for being absent during my childhood. He was doing a really good job, but I didn't tell him that. I enjoyed being babied and spoiled by him.

"Who the hell is Houston?" I asked, making sure I hadn't been dreaming when Sassy spewed her load of crap.

"Youse are," Fat Bastard announced, hopping up on my bed and planting his furry and very large ass in my lap.

"No. I'm not."

"Would you prefer Dallas?" Fabdudio inquired, looking puzzled.

"No."

"Austin?" Baba Yaga suggested.

"Galveston?" Mac tried one out.

"Fort Worth?" Marge *aka* Cookie Witch added.

"San Antonio?" Jeeves the Kangaroo shifter *aka* Sassy's husband *aka* Mac's adopted son chimed in.

"No. No. No. And oh my Goddess, no," I replied with an eye roll. "Sassy's confused… as usual. I'm still going by Zelda."

"Wait," Sassy yelled in her outdoor voice, making all in the room wince in pain. "Were you speaking Chinese when you said all that stuff?"

Now everyone was confused—except me.

"Yes. Yes, I was speaking Chinese."

"Goddess, what a relief," Sassy said, flopping down on the bed next to me. "For a minute there I thought I was losing my newfound brilliance. I'm clearly going to have to learn to speak Chinese."

"That would probably be helpful," I said with the smallest eye roll I could manage without getting busted.

"So do you think you might have been speaking Chinese when you did the spell?" Sassy asked. "You know the Goddess might not understand Chinese either and therefore thought you wanted Roger to have a pentagon of penises."

"I'm sorry," Cookie Witch choked out with her hand over her mouth. "Did you just say *pentagon of penises*?"

"I most certainly did," Sassy huffed, totally offended. "*Pentagon* means five for everyone's information. It's a French word. Roger now has five love muscles. So it stands to reason that he has a pentagon of penii. You feel me?"

"She kind of has a point in a rather unorthodox way," Jeeves admitted, standing up for his deranged wife.

"But a pentagon is a shape with five connected sides," Fabio said, bending over at the waist clearly feeling phantom pain for Roger. "Does it actually *look* like a pentagon? Are they connected?"

"Dat would be sumpin' to see," Jango Fett said, scratching his kitty head with his paw. "Youse would have a hard time takin' a leak if the giggle sticks was connected."

The room went silent. I felt like passing out again. Did Roger have a pentagon in his pants or just five unconnected man bits? Goddess, the images were endless and gross. I was definitely going back to the pokey for this one—even *I* thought I deserved time in the big house for this mess.

"Umm… what does a pentagon actually look like?" Sassy asked, looking somewhat bewildered.

With a wave of her hand, Marge produced a drawing of a pentagon and gave it to Sassy. Sassy studied the picture thirty-seven seconds too long for my sanity.

"Nope, it doesn't look like this," she announced to a very relieved audience. "Looks more like a hand and finger weenies with balls."

"Well, that certainly makes it all better," I snapped, shoving Fat Bastard off my lap and Sassy off my bed.

Hopping to my feet, I began to pace the room. I knew I was coming unhinged, but this was horrifying. Roger must be a basket case. He was always a slight basket case, but this… this would make a sane rabbit a freakin' mess.

"I have to fix it," I muttered, pacing like a caged tiger hopped up on a vat of caffeine and multiple boxes of Twinkies. "I really didn't want to touch it, but I'm going to have to. Maybe if I wear gloves I won't puke on him. I mean, it would be bad if I hurled on him after I gave him a pants-full of peckers. And who ever even heard of a spell going *this* wrong? It's appalling. I'm completely willing to hand myself over to the authorities and go back to the pokey. I just want you all to make sure my children know how much I love them and don't tell them why I had to live out my life doing hard time until they're at least thirty… or fifty… or never. Just make something up that sounds good. The only thing I request is that I don't have to wear orange. It clashes so badly with my hair, I don't think I would survive it. Do you all feel me here?"

"Zelda, calm down," Baba Yaga snapped in a brook no bullshit voice.

I was actually relieved she was so bossy until I looked over at her and lost the use of speech.

She was dressed in sunshine yellow spandex from head to toe. Her wrists were adorned with so many black rubber bracelets, I figured she could bounce or float on water. The silver sequined cone-shaped bra over the unitard could put an eye out. But the gauzy purple skirt trimmed in feathers and tiny pictures of Madonna's face was the topper—from hell.

Baba Yaga, *aka* Carol, was working an enormous hairdo that must have taken ten cans of hairspray to hold up and her eyes were rimmed with yellow glitter. The most shocking part of all was that even though the woman looked like a reject from a Madonna video, she was still gorgeous.

Unreal.

As much as I wanted the voice of reason to tell me what to do, it was going to be difficult to make eye contact with her and not laugh.

"Trying," I said, staring at her nose. It was the only thing on her face that didn't sparkle. "I'm just going to have to reverse the spell."

"Bad idea," Marge said.

Thankfully Marge had taste and was easy on the eye. She and Baba Yaga were sisters and looked alarmingly alike, but Marge wasn't permanently stuck in the eighties.

"Why?" I asked. "I gave him too many John Holmeses with a spell. I can take them away with a spell."

"What exactly does John Holmes have to do with this?" Marge asked with tremendous trepidation.

She feared my answer—as well she should.

However, Sassy decided to take over and we all became terrified.

"There was a genitalia—another French word or possibly Swedish—naming ceremony about a year ago," Sassy informed an increasingly pale Marge. "Roger admitted he named his member John Holmes—which I have to say is *wildly inaccurate*. Anyhoo, Zelda is just avoiding having to come up with polite penis terms by calling Roger's wang by its proper name."

"I see," Marge said, pressing the bridge of her nose and biting back either laughter or bile.

"So I say we just decide on one single name for the salami and this will all go much smoother," Sassy suggested as if that would solve the heinous fact that I'd more than doubled Roger's *salami*.

"I put my vote in for rod, tallywhacker or dong. Youse can't go wrong with dem names," Boba Fett volunteered.

"Youse is forgettin' 100% beef thermometer, The General and pork sword," Fat Bastard added.

"Nah, youse guys got it all wrong. I'd go for tent pole or meat popsicle," Jango Fett rounded out the disgusting suggestion pile.

"How about this?" I stated calmly as I waved my hand and rendered my revolting familiars mute.

"Thank you," Marge said. "However, until we get to the bottom of what happened, I don't think you should use magic, Zelda."

"That's kind of harsh," Sassy commented, coming to my defense.

It was harsh—really harsh, but Marge was right. I'd used dark magic on Roger and didn't even realize it was happening. Goddess only knew what other tragedies I could conjure up.

Twisting my hair in my fingers, I sighed and plopped back down on the bed. "Marge is right," I said, defeated. "I'm a danger to myself and others right now. If I keep going like this, we could have a town of seventy-five people with enough genitalia for three hundred."

Thankfully no one had a comment for that. I don't think I would have been able to stop myself from zapping someone who agreed with my grim statement.

"She needs to be trained," Baba Yaga stated the obvious. "If Zelda can't control the dark, it will control her."

"And who exactly is going to train her?" Mac asked, not liking the direction of the conversation any more than I did.

"Has to be someone who has dark magic," Fabio said.

"I have dark magic," Sassy announced with a shudder. "However, I'd like to go on record now saying I have no fucking idea how to use it either. And in solidarity—pretty sure that's a German word—with my best friend Zelda, I'm not going to use magic either. If she gave Roger five… wait, what did we decide to call them?"

"We didn't," Jeeves told her.

"Okay then I'm just going to randomly pick a name. Cool?"

When no one answered she took that as a yes.

"If Zelda *aka Houston* gave Roger five badoinkadoinks, I'm liable to saddle someone with ten to twenty. That would be a total shit show and pants would be a real problem. I don't even know if pants would be a possibility and since winter is coming… well, you all get my drift. Right?"

"Unfortunately we do," Baba Yaga said, shaking her head. "I think it's best if you don't say anything else for at least thirty minutes, Sassy."

"Is that an order or suggestion?" Sassy asked.

"Order," everyone in the room said in unison.

"There's really only one option," Marge said as her lovely face turned pink with embarrassment.

"And that is?" Mac asked.

"We bring Bermangoggleshitz to Assjacket," Marge announced.

"My dad?" Sassy asked, clearly forgetting she wasn't supposed to speak. "Here? In Assjacket?"

Baba Yaga nodded her head and watched her sister with interest. "Yes. I agree. He's working on redeeming himself. This might be just the thing for him to prove he's serious about becoming a better warlock."

"I don't like it one bit," Mac said through gritted teeth.

"Neither do I," Fabio said. "But I have to agree with Marge and Carol on this one. He's the only one to train the girls to use the dark sorcery without hurting themselves or anyone else."

"And you think he'll do it?" Mac growled. "He'll play by the rules?"

"He wants something here," Baba Yaga said, still staring at her sister. "So yes, I believe he will abide by any conditions we set. And if he doesn't, I will end him."

"You can do that? You can kill him?" I asked taken by surprise.

"I'm the Baba fucking Yaga," she said with a wide grin. "I can do whatever I want. Plus there are many things far worse than death, my child."

"Yeah," I muttered, leaning on Mac for support. "Five badoinkadoinks is one of those things."

"Trust me," Baba Yaga said. "Roger is a bit… how can I put this politely… pervy. He'll be more disappointed when he's back to one than he is devastated that he has five."

"I hope you're right," I said, closing my eyes and breathing in the delicious scent of my mate. Mac's presence alone gave me strength.

All I wanted to do was curl up into a ball and pretend today hadn't happened. I wanted to play with my babies and then act out a pornographic fairy tale with Mac when the kids went to bed…

But all that would have to wait. I had penance to pay. And pay it I would.

Shitshitshitshit.

CHAPTER FOUR

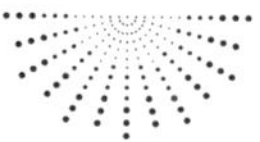

"What are you doing?" Sassy asked watching me with great interest.

"Laundry," I mumbled, wondering how much soap I was supposed to add. Living without magic was almost more of a shit show than living with it. I was a freakin' disaster in the home department. I'd used too much soap in the dishwasher this morning and gave the kitchen a bubble bath by accident.

Henry and Audrey had been delighted. Me? Not so much. Thankfully Fabio had been here and was able to magically erase my bubbly booboo.

"Those have some nasty stains," Sassy pointed out, referring to the onesies my babies had worn on the outing with their dad.

They had shifted into wolf puppies and I'd missed it due to the horrifying fact I'd been busy giving Roger multiple badoinkadoinks. I was heartbroken that I'd been absent for their first shift, but they'd been shifting constantly at home now. It was all kinds of unreal and they were just as cute as tiny wolves as they were babies.

"Yep," I agreed, staring helplessly at the grass stains on the knees of the adorable little outfits. "I think I saw on Pinterest that you're supposed to soak grass stained clothes to get them clean."

"In what? Vodka?"

"Not sure… maybe toothpaste," I said. "Or lemon juice and hydrogen peroxide with some fertilizer."

"Do you have all that stuff?" Sassy asked.

"No."

"Should I go get your dad? He's downstairs with Henry and Audrey teaching them how to play blackjack."

"Like my dad knows how to do laundry?" I snapped with an enormous eye roll.

"Point."

"Exactly. He's doing enough damage teaching my kids to play poker."

Sassy paused and I could see the wheels of her pea brain turning. It was all kinds of unsettling.

"Then I say we just throw them out and get new shit."

That gave me pause. She had a fine point, but that was the weenie way out. I wasn't a weenie… Nope. I just created weenies. Lots of them. Shitballs. I needed to remove all penis references from my vocabulary. It was too depressing to constantly relive my massive fuck up.

Thankfully Baba Yaga was correct. Roger was delighted with his *enhancement*. He'd sent flowers and cookies. However, I was still so mortified at the mess I'd made I couldn't even eat one cookie. And I freakin' loved cookies.

"We're not throwing them out. Just because we have no skills doesn't mean we can't learn them. Can you pull up Pinterest on your phone?"

"Don't have a phone."

"Why not?"

"You blew it up," Sassy reminded me.

Motherhumpin' crapballs. She was correct. And the Goddess

only knew where my phone was. If my head wasn't attached to my body I would have lost that too.

"Okay. Fine. This is not a problem," I said, sounding far more confident than I felt. "I'm just gonna fill up the utility sink and put some dryer sheets in there and seven caps of detergent."

"Should I get some vodka?" Sassy inquired.

"No, the kids are underage. I don't want them to smell like a bar. But go get the toothpaste from my bathroom. I want to smear it all over the stains before we soak them."

"Sounds like a plan," Sassy said, skipping out of the laundry room.

"Probably a bad plan," I muttered to no one since I was alone now.

Feeling worthless, I sat down on the mountainous pile of dirty towels and let my head drop to my hands. I was a disaster as a witch and clearly a disaster as a human. I didn't know how to do anything without magic. Not to mention, if Roger's new additions were any indication, I didn't know what to do *with* magic either...

And now Bermangoggleshitz was coming to train me. Life kept getting suckier.

Well, I could still love Mac and my babies. I didn't need magic for that. Audrey and Henry didn't seem to mind that I wasn't using enchantment to float their stuffed animals around the room or make the pictures in their storybooks pop off the page and play with them. They were simply happy to be with me.

But they were babies. They didn't know I was a magical megaflop.

"The toothpaste has arrived!" Sassy announced with an armload of bathroom products.

Biting back my grin, I heaved myself up to see what other potions she'd grabbed. "Have you researched any of this?" I asked, taking a few bath bombs and a bottle of shampoo out of her hands.

"No, but it stands to reason that they should work. If this shit can clean teeth, hair and bodies, it should be able to get rid of pesky grass stains—that was Greek," she explained as she dumped the contents into the utility sink.

"What was Greek?" I asked, adding the dryer sheets and seven caps of detergent to the brew.

"Pesky. Comes from the word Peskodopolis, meaning jackhole."

It was difficult to render me speechless. Hard, but doable. Sassy was a pro at it.

Together we stared at the goopy mess in the sink. It didn't look quite right to me, but what did I know? Apparently nothing. At least I was trying. Mac was proud of me and that made me feel ten feet tall.

"Do we just leave it?" Sassy asked.

"I think we need to add water," I said, wildly unsure. "At least it smells good."

"Hot or cold?" she asked, hands on the knobs.

"I'm gonna go with both," I replied and then froze.

They yelp from the Great Room didn't sound good. Thankfully it wasn't Henry or Audrey. It sounded more like Fat Bastard, but I wasn't sure. Without a backward glance, I sprinted out of the laundry room like a demon was on my heels. No, I couldn't use magic, but I would protect my children with everything I had left. Always.

"It ain't no big deal, Sugar Boots," Fat Bastard said with my son in baby wolf form attached to his big hairy butt. "We was wrestlin' and baby Henry here got hisself a little excited."

"Henry," I said, ignoring my cat's strange endearment while trying not to laugh at the bizarre picture of my child with his fangs embedded in my rotund familiar's butt. "We don't bite people *or* cats. Take your teeth out of Fat Bastard's rear end and shift back to human. Now."

With a little huff and a shrill giggle from his sister, Henry shifted and crawled over to me. My twins were ten months old. They were a fabulously joyful handful, but I refused to raise heathens who bit others in the ass.

Scooping him up and snuggling him close, I breathed him in. "That's not what a good boy does," I told him. "We do not bite people. Ever. Am I clear?"

Taking the big wet smackaroo to my cheek as a yes, I sat him down on the floor with Audrey. My other two familiars, Jango Fett and Boba Fett along with Lucky and Charm—my babies' little kitten familiars—were busy checking out Fat Bastard's ass.

"Doll Face," Fat Bastard said with a wide and proud grin on his feline face. "Don't youse be getting' down on the boy. Weeze was teachin' him how to defend hisself. Magic don't always work. Sometimes youse gotta use manpower—or in his case—motherhumpin' sharp, pointy, little fang power."

"They're *babies*," I said, stressing the word so they would know I meant business. "They do not need to learn how to fight before they walk. And I *don't* want them to think it's okay to bite people."

"What about bad guys?" Jango asked. "Youse gotta want 'em to smack down on bad motherfuckers. Right?"

"Dooze not say fucker in front of the rugrats," Fat Bastard hissed and walloped Jango in the back of the head.

"My bad," Jango said, getting in a quick left kitty hook to The Bastard's jiggly gut. "I meant mother farker... which is very different from motherfucker."

"Clearly," I said with an eye roll to beat all eye rolls.

"I was here the entire time," Fabio chimed in as if *that* was supposed to reassure me...

My father patted Henry and Audrey on their heads full of curly red hair as they giggled happily.

"Yep, I also heard you were teaching them how to gamble," I said, giving my dad the *look*.

Fabio had gotten in tremendous amounts of trouble gambling over his centuries on earth and was trying to change his ways…

"It's good to learn early so you don't get screwed over," Fabio pointed out with a sheepish shrug. "Anyway, they got bored with cards so we played horsey."

"Horsey?"

"Yep," Jango bellowed and fell over in exhaustion. "Weeze was the horseys and the babies was the cowboys."

Chuckling, I shook my head. Jango didn't have far to fall as his enormous stomach almost touched the ground. My children's upbringing was definitely odd, but it was also full of love—the exact opposite of mine. So if my cats wanted to be horseys and my dad wanted to play cards, I was okay with it.

"Let me see your butt," I said to Fat Bastard, gently pushing all the cats out of the way and examining him. "I need to heal that."

"Umm… you can't," Sassy reminded me with waggling eyebrows while miming male genitalia with her hands.

And yet another fail for me.

My eyes filled with tears and I stared at my feet. This was awful.

"It ain't nothin'" Fat Bastard assured me. "A band-aid, some scotch and a good Cuban cigar will fix my ass up just fine."

"Come with me to my office," I said. "Maybe I can do a little something without magic to make you feel better."

"And just so youse know, Sweet Cheeks, I'm fine with an extra pecker or three," my cat said over his shoulder as he waddled his fat ass out the front door followed by his equally rotund cohorts.

"I'm never going to live this one down, am I?" I said.

"Nope," Fabio confirmed with a grin on his handsome face. "You want me to watch the little ones?"

"Are you going to teach them anything illegal?" I countered.

"Umm… no?"

"Yes, I want you to watch them, and no, you will not teach them anything illegal. They need a nap soon anyway."

"Do you have Windex?" Sassy asked, hopping up and down in excitement.

"What's Windex?" I asked.

"She does," Fabio said with a chuckle. "Under the sink. Why?"

"Didn't any of you people see *My Big Fat Greek Wedding*?" Sassy demanded, trying to open the cabinet. "What in the Goddess's name is wrong with your cabinet?"

"Child guards," I said, flicking the latch so Sassy could find this Windex she was so fixated on.

"Those are awesome," she said, ransacking the cleaning stuff I didn't know I had under my sink. "I'm gonna have to get some for my house to lock up my vibrators. My kids think they're back massagers. So did you see the movie?"

"No," Fabio and I answered in unison and then a matching gag at Sassy's overshare.

"Oh my Goddess," she screeched so loud I was sure my eardrum was damaged. "You have to see it. Anyhoo, Windex is magic human liquid. Heals all kinds of shit."

"Seriously?"

"Totally."

Maybe today was looking up…

Or maybe not.

CHAPTER FIVE

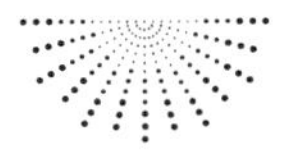

"Okay, hold still," I said to Fat Bastard as I prepared to spray his ass with Windex.

I wasn't sure I believed Sassy, but since I was working at a disadvantage I figured it couldn't hurt… much.

"Jeeze," Fat Bastard yelled as he winced, jumped three feet in the air, and then fell off the examining table with a thud. "What are youse trying to do here? Remove my ass?"

"Youse gots a huge ass," Jango commented, enjoying the show immensely. "Youse could use a reduction."

"Say dat again," Fat Bastard hissed.

"I said, youse gots a…"

And that was all Jango got out before Fat Bastard launched his corpulent carcass at his partner in crime. The hissing and swearing was outrageous. If it wasn't so destructive to my pretty office space, I would have laughed at my pudgy felines having a smackdown.

"Enough," I shouted coming this close to using my forbidden magic.

The fat fuckers ignored me. Not happening. They didn't want to listen? Fine.

Not. A. Problem.

Brandishing my Windex, I found an opening and went in. I pumped that trigger like I was a freakin' gunslinger in the old west.

And it worked. It really was human magic juice.

"Motherhumper in a fuckin' jockstrap with jock itch," Fat Bastard shrieked. "Youse made me blind."

"I'm squeakin'" Jango shouted. "What the ever lovin' jackhole is dat shit?"

"Windex," I replied with my finger still on the trigger. "And I'll use it again if you two asshats keep fighting."

"Weeze are done," Jango confirmed as he dragged his squeaky body to the exit. "Dat shit is evil."

"Smells like Boba's ass in August," Fat Bastard commented as he went to town on his nuts to remove the offending scent.

"I present dat," Boba Fett grunted as he sharpened his claws in preparation for a brawl. "Youse gots an ass that smells like a garbage truck full of dead bodies."

"Don't you mean resent?" I asked, slightly confused.

"S'what I said," Boba shot back.

"Say dat again, youse atomic turd fungus," Fat Bastard snarled.

"Wit pleasure, youse moist knob buccaneer."

"Nope," I shouted, aiming the blue bottle at them. "Do not ever say *moist* again. I will make you drink this shit if you do. I *hate* that word—I mean the rest of it was gross too, but the M word is *not* okay." I was not going to break up another cat smackdown with magic human juice. Besides the cats were correct. It did smell funky. "All of you jackwads are leaving. Bermangoggleshitz is arriving soon. I don't want you to beat the hell out of each other unnecessarily. You feel me?"

"Youse got it Sugar Socks," Fat Bastard grumbled, flipping his kitty middle figure at his two buddies. "Weeze will get cleaned up and be back."

"What about his butt?" Sassy asked, pointed at the Bastard's still injured ass.

My brain raced to find a solution. This was not the way things were supposed to be. As much as I didn't want to deal with Bermangoggleshitz, I knew I needed him. I had a job to do and I couldn't do it. Crap.

"I don't know," I admitted in a small voice.

"I have an idea," Sassy announced.

The cats froze in fear and I inched my way toward the exit just incase her idea included an explosion.

"Will we survive it?" I asked, keeping my voice as neutral as possible.

"Yesssssss," she said with a giggle. "Your dad is a healer warlock. All you gorgeous redheaded witches are healers. So, I say until you're able to do magic that doesn't include bestowing multiple dongs, your dad can heal the Shifters."

Sassy was brilliant—simply brilliant. Even my cats were impressed.

All redheaded witches *were* healers and we were rare. The witches were stronger than the warlocks in the healing department, but my dad could definitely take care of our people until I got a grip on my dark magic.

Sassy was the walking definition of idiotic brilliance and I adored her for it.

"You can pick three things from my closet," I told my BFF.

"And I can keep them?" she squealed.

"Yes," I said, not even caring if she took the Birkin bag.

I was maturing… kind of… plus I had every intention of hiding my newest Birkin.

CHAPTER SIX

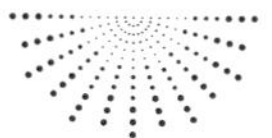

Well, he looked a *little* better than the last time I'd seen him, although that wasn't really saying much. The horns were still there. Half of his face was otherworldly beautiful and the other half was still kind of the stuff nightmares were made of. I did have to admit his looks had improved somewhat in the months since I'd last seen him at Sassy's wedding to Jeeves.

Bermangoggleshitz was enormous and built like a brick shithouse. He had one crystal clear blue eye and the other was still beady black. His hair was blond like Sassy's and the good half of him looked like her.

The bad half? Not so much.

However, it did appear that the good half was winning out. At least I prayed to the Goddess it was. I didn't need anymore trouble than I already had.

"Those are harsh terms, considering you people need me," Bermangoggleshitz said, leaning back in his chair and eyeing the occupants in the office.

No one moved a muscle—not Sassy, Mac, Marge or me. Baba Yaga was running the show at the moment and she was kicking some witchy ass. I was a little concerned that her outfit would negate her upper hand, but thankfully I was wrong. She was dressed head to toe in silver lamé and was even wearing a freakin' rhinestone crown. I decided not to look at her. It was be all kinds of stupid for me to laugh at a time like this.

We'd decided to hold the gathering in my office on the far side of our property as opposed to our house. I wanted to keep my children as far from Roy Bermangoggleshitz as possible at the moment. He didn't need to know anything about my babies and their Goddess given powers at the moment.

In fact, I wanted to keep them a secret from the magical world as long as possible. They could in no way defend themselves yet. Once the word got out there would be unwelcome *interest* from every corner of the Universe.

"The terms stand, *Roy*," Baba Yaga said in a cool tone as she filed her nails. "If you want to stay, you will play by them."

"And if I don't, *Carol*?" he inquired, staring daggers at the leader of the magical world as he laughed at her.

The use of her name was disrespectful, but his laugh made her eyes narrow to slits.

Baba dropped her file to the ground and slowly crossed the room to stand right in front of Barmangoggleshtz's chair. Looking down at him she smiled. It wasn't pretty and it scared the shit out of me and everyone else in attendance.

"If you don't, you can say goodbye to your daughter for good —not to mention everyone else in the room," she purred in a voice so icy even Bermangoggleshitz shivered.

Baba had him by the balls. Bermangoggleshitz had made it abundantly clear that he wanted to be in Sassy's life. The only reason he looked as good as he did—good being a *very* relative word—was that he'd made some major fucking changes to deserve Sassy's love.

Not to mention he had it really bad for Marge...

"Fine," he snapped. "I'll abide by your terms, but I have some of my own—and they're non- negotiable."

Baba circled the room sparkling like a freaking disco ball as she considered Roy's ultimatum. She didn't like backtalk. I knew this first hand. However, we needed Bermangoggleshitz.

She knew it and he knew it.

"State them," she said flatly.

"When I train the girls in dark magic, I'm in charge. No questions asked."

Mac growled deep in his throat. He wasn't happy about that, and to be honest it made me a bit uncomfortable as well, but Baba didn't seem fazed.

"Fine. What else?" she questioned.

"I shall need a *keeper* here. It will make all of you *people* more comfortable... and it will please me."

"And who would that keeper be?" Baba Yaga inquired as she picked up her file and began shaping her nails again as if our lives and future weren't on the line.

His pause was dramatic and I had a very bad feeling I knew exactly what he was about to say.

"Marge shall be my keeper," Bermangoggleshitz said with a shrug of his shoulders and a grin that almost made him look attractive.

"No," Marge hissed. "Absolutely not."

Her eyes narrowed, her long blonde hair blew wildly around her head and her fingers began to spark. She was magnificent and pretty damned scary.

"My terms are non-negotiable," he said calmly, staring at her with very little emotion on his face. "Take them or leave them. I have other things that could be occupying my time and I'd be delighted to leave. Your choice... *Marge*."

Without even a glance at Marge, Baba Yaga nodded her head. "We accept your terms."

"Are you insane?" Marge yelled at her sister.

"That's kind of a given," I muttered under my breath. "The outfit is a dead giveaway."

"Heard that," Baba said, flicking her fingers and zapping my ass.

"Shit," I shouted as I smacked out the fire on my butt. Now my dad was going to have to heal Fat Bastard and me.

"This is a bad plan," Marge insisted, avoiding all eye contact with Bermangoggleshitz and getting right up in her sister's face. "I don't have time for this foolishness."

"Time becomes meaningless when you live as long as we do. And foolishness is a very relative word," Baba Yaga told Marge as she gently touched her sister's flushed cheek. "Time marches on and there is very little we can do about it except live in the moment—and those, too are fleeting, my sister. You have hidden yourself away for far too long. If you don't grow some goddessdamned balls and live your life, I shall have to force you to do so."

"Zelda could whip her up some balls," Sassy volunteered.

"I was speaking metaphorically, Sassy," Baba Yaga said with her eyes still focused on Marge.

"Is that Chinese?" Sassy inquired, getting annoyed.

"Yes," I inserted quickly before Sassy gave up her ban on using magic and blew up my beautiful office with all of us in it.

"So Marge, *darling*," Bermangoggleshitz said in a horridly self-satisfied tone, knowing he'd won. "We shall stay at your place."

"I don't have one," she snapped, giving him such a withering glare, I wondered how long it would take old Roy to regret his demand.

"She lives with me and it's kinda tight," Sassy announced. "It's me, Jeeves, Marge and the boys—Chad, Chip, Chunk and Chutney. But since you *are* my dad, I can make you a bed up in the kitchen. However, you should know that my boys wake up at dawn's buttcrack and watching them eat is like sitting through a horror movie. The only saving grace is that they don't eat meat—hence no blood… unless you take their gum and nuts away. And by nuts, I don't mean testicles. If they can't chew on something, they'll cannibalize their own faces. Very unappetizing.

"Is there an inn in town?" Bermangoggleshitz asked, looking dazed and confused from his daughter's monologue.

"Nope," I said. "I have a tree house, but it's my floating nookie hut. Not sure how weird that would get. You feel me?"

"No, I actually didn't understand a word of that," Bermangoggleshitz replied, appearing even more dazed. "Maybe it would be fine at Sassy's."

"Don't forget Marge, Jeeves and the boys," Sassy reminded him.

Sassy had adopted four grown chipmunk Shifters who'd tried to kill me. Well, actually they were vegetarians and couldn't hurt a flea. They would have never harmed me. The gum-smacking weirdos had been in big trouble and in the end I'd forgiven them for attempted murder and welcomed them into the Assjacket fold.

Of course, Sassy had one upped me and adopted the wiry haired little freaks.

"So I guess it's not going to work out," Marge said, with over exaggerated sadness. "Sorry, Charlie."

"His name is Roy," Sassy whispered to Marge.

"I know, I was just… never mind," Marge said. "I was speaking Chinese."

"I thought so," Sassy said, nodded her blonde curls.

"You will stay here," Baba Yaga announced.

"In my office?" I asked, shocked. I loved my office and it was mine.

"Seeing as you have little use for it *at the moment*," Baba said with a raised brow. "I would think you would offer up the hospitality—especially since you'd like to be able to use it again. You *feel* me? Plus, it's on your property. It will be quick to get to for training."

Goddess, I hated it when the crazy old bag was correct. Unless

I got a grip on my dark magic, I wasn't going to be able to heal people—hence no need for the gorgeous office that Mac had built for me.

Shit.

"Yes," I said slowly and somewhat ungraciously. "I'd be delighted to let Bermangoggleshitmypants stay here."

"What did you just call me?" Bermangoggleshitz asked, clearly displeased.

"I'm not sure."

"It was Chinese," Sassy informed her father.

Bermangoggleshitz stared at me until I felt itchy. Maybe I would be a bit more subtle in the future.

"No worries," Bermangoggleshitz said with a chuckle that was all kinds of scary. "Zelda will pay for her impertinence."

"Don't be a dick," Sassy warned her dad.

Bermangoggleshitz paused and pressed his temples dramatically. "Darling," he said to his daughter. "I'm trying here—for you. But dick is fairly second nature to me, so I can't guarantee outstanding behavior."

"How about acceptable behavior?" Sassy countered.

"Define acceptable," he countered back in all seriousness.

"I don't care if you're a dick," I said calmly. I refused to let the skanky warlock know he unnerved me. "It gives me free rein to be a dick right back."

Bermangoggleshitz raised his brow and then grinned. "You are truly refreshing."

"However," I added not wanting to be *too* refreshing… that grin was kind of nightmare inducing. "If you're extremely dickish, I'll be compelled to use my out of control magical pentagonal mojo on you."

"What language are you speaking?" Bermangoggleshitz asked with an eye roll.

"Chinese," Sassy informed him. "I'm learning it, so don't worry your partially hideous head about it. I figure in a few weeks, months or years I'll be fluent—which is a Spanish word in case you were wondering—and I can interpret for you. Cool?"

After that the semi-evil warlock went mute. Sassy was actually one of the most powerful weapons we had—magic or no magic.

"Oh," Sassy continued, oblivious to her father's utter bewilderment. "Zelda or *Houston* as she sometimes goes by because of Apollo 13—which I haven't seen—gave Roger five wanks. So I'd suggest that unless you want to risk having your pants full of peens, you should watch your mouth. And just so we're clear... Five badoinkadoinks would mean you couldn't wear pants. You're already working at a very unpopular disadvantage here and I would think streaking with multiple dongs would make you seriously friendless."

"I'm so confused," Bermangoggleshitz whispered.

"Join the club," Baba Yaga said. "She's your daughter."

"So what's the plan?" Sassy asked, completely unaware of the head scratching discombobulating mess she'd caused.

"You will start your training tomorrow," Baba Yaga announced. "Roy and Marge will stay here and I will go home."

I gaped at our leader and slapped my hands on my hips. "You're shitting me."

"Do you eat with that mouth?" Baba asked with a raised brow.

"She does," Sassy confirmed.

"Sassy's correct," I added. "You can't just leave."

Baba Yaga paused and stared at me. Slowly an evil slash delighted little grin spread across her glittery lips. "So you're ready to take over my job?"

"Absofuckinglutely not," I snapped.

"Well then, until you are, you're not the boss of me. Am I clear?" she asked, beginning to spark like a firework.

"As mud," I mumbled.

"Excellent," Baba Yaga trilled, deciding to give me a pass on my rude comment. "There's a little wrinkle problem that needs my attention at the moment."

"I'd offer to iron it, but I blasted that motherhumpin' piece of metal straight to hell," Sassy announced. "I was ironing the boy's underpants and my phone rang. I went to answer it because Jeeves usually calls during his lunch break and we have phone sex. Well, wouldn't you just fucking know, I answered the iron and singed off half the hair on my head."

"Should I gag her?" I muttered, shaking my head and trying not to laugh.

"No," Baba Yaga said quickly. "If she overshares one more time, I want the honor. Sassy, a wrinkle is a time warp of sorts. One can hide in them. It's how Marge stayed hidden for years and now something hideous has figured out how to use them."

"Like Demons?' Sassy asked. "Those assbags are certainly hideous—Japanese word for those of you wondering."

"Hideous is Japanese?" Bermagoggleshitz asked, baffled.

"No," Sassy told her dumbfounded father. "*Assbag* is Japanese."

Always good for her word, Baba Yaga flicked her fingers and covered Sassy's mouth with glittering duct tape. Then there was about twenty-two seconds of silence while we tried to remember what we'd actually been talking about. Marge got there first.

"Demons are using wrinkles to come to Earth?" Marge asked, appalled but getting us back on track.

Bermangoggleshitz growled and his one still ugly eye glowed red. "The Demons are back?"

"We kicked those fuckers back to hell," I said with a shudder. All I needed right now was to have to deal with the underworld while I was a menace to my own world.

"No," Baba Yaga said, shaking her head slowly. "Not Demons. However, I'm not quite sure who or what it is, but they're using the wrinkles for nefarious purposes. I plan to find the culprits and destroy them."

"I'm coming with you," Marge said. "I understand wrinkles better than most."

Baba Yaga shook her head again and kissed her sister's cheek. "You're needed here. You will stay."

"I don't like this," Mac said through clenched teeth. "Do you think it might be Vampires?"

"Possibly, but trust me... I will take care of it and it won't be pretty. I have a sneaking suspicion it might be a little closer to home than expected. No worries. I've got it under control," Baba Yaga said in a tone that made me believe every word she said.

"Closer to home?" Marge pressed. "Whose home? Do you know more?"

Baba Yaga shrugged and gave her sister a terse smile. "Just a hunch. So," she went on turning from scary witch to cruise director on a dime. "We shall leave Marge and Roy to get reacquainted and you people will reconvene tomorrow at nine AM sharp."

Marge said nothing, but if the venomous glare she shot at Roy was anything to go by I actually felt a little sorry for him. Cookie Witch didn't suffer fools gladly.

I was pretty sure Bermangoggleshitz was a fool.

Thankfully, not my problem.

Well, at least not till tomorrow morning...

CHAPTER SEVEN

"Oh my Goddess," I screeched as I spied Fabio and my babies tearing toward us through the woods at a fast clip. Henry and Audrey were in wolf form and Fabio was huffing and puffing trying to keep up with them. "Something's wrong."

We'd left Marge and Roy just as Marge was drawing a line with permanent marker across the lobby of my office—delineating her side from his. It was going to take some work to restore my beautiful office once we were done with Bermangoggleshitz.

However, my worries about my office could wait. My kids and dad came first.

"What happened?" Mac demanded, scooping Henry and Audrey into his arms and holding them tight.

"You have an indoor pool," Fabio said breathlessly, trying not to laugh.

He failed.

"No we don't," I said.

"Could have fooled me."

I got a horrible sinking feeling in my stomach. I wasn't exactly sure what I'd done, but I was positive it wasn't good.

"Actually," Fabio continued. "It's more like a massive, indoor, floor-to-ceiling tub—all bubbly and strangely minty fresh."

"Shit," I screamed and then slapped my hand over my potty mouth. I really hoped Henry and Audrey's first word wasn't *shit*...

"Goddess in plaid gauchos," Sassy echoed my horror. "I forgot to turn off the sink in the laundry room. I am sooooooo sorry."

I started to laugh. If I didn't laugh, I would cry. Sassy and I were epic fails in the domestic department.

"It's okay. It's my fault too," I said, shaking my head.

"No, it's my fault," Sassy said. "I take full responsibility and I'll clean it up—by hand—since I gave up magic for a few-ish days. I'll also return the Birkin bags I legally took from your closet. You didn't hide that new one very well."

"No," Mac said so loudly, we all jumped. "No. While the sentiment is lovely, the reality is horrifying. I'll call a few friends and we'll get it cleaned up."

"You found the tan Birkin?" I asked, surprised.

She nodded and smirked. "I can sniff out a Birkin within five miles."

"Damn, you're good."

"I know. Right?" Sassy giggled and bowed.

"How about this?" Fabio suggested. "I'll use a little voodoo and clean up the catastrophe if Zelda and Sassy promise not to touch anything electrical or anything that has plumbing attached to it."

Sassy raised her hand and waited patiently to be called on.

"Sassy?" Fabio asked with a slight wince. "Do you have a question?"

"I do. What about vibrators?"

Fabio looked pained. Mac looked up to the Heavens and appeared to be praying for strength and my babies giggled. I hoped like hell they couldn't understand what numbnuts had just asked.

"Umm… how about we just lay off everything electronic for a few days," Fabio suggested gamely.

"Will do," Sassy said with a salute to my dad. "Jeeves might be a little put out because…"

"TMI," I shouted. "That is entirely too much information, Sassy."

"My bad."

"Okay, anymore questions?" Fabio asked with a hint of fear in his voice.

Sassy raised her hand again and we all ignored it.

"Great! No more questions," Fabio said, studiously examining his fingernails. "No electronics. No plumbing. No indoor swimming pools."

"I can work with that," I replied sheepishly. "But the house will be a mess."

"Messes are fine," Mac said, kissing the top of my head. "I really don't want to have to replace our home."

"Can I use my cell phone?" Sassy asked.

"You don't have one anymore," I reminded her.

"Right," she said, slapping her forehead. "Problem solved."

"So what's the plan?" Fabio inquired as we began to make our way back to our flooded abode.

"We start training with Bermangogglesnot tomorrow morning. Marge is staying with the freak at my office and your *gal pal* left to take care of a wrinkle issue," I told my dad.

"Interesting. I shall have to talk with my *gal pal*. Don't like her conquering the world on her own," he replied, tilting his handsome head and taking the information in. "Marge was probably *thrilled* about staying with her old flame."

Mac laughed. "Understatement. Roy's gonna be lucky to leave Assjacket with his balls in one piece."

"Not a problem," Sassy chimed in as she did a cartwheel and landed on her ass, much to my children's delight. "Zelda can give him ten before he goes home."

"Goddess in a tutu and Crocs," I groused. "I'm never gonna live Roger's *enhancement* down."

"Nope," Fabio replied with a wide grin. "You've given us ammunition for centuries."

Just. Fucking. Awesome.

I just prayed to the Goddess that Bermangogglebutthole could teach me to control my dark magic quickly so I didn't have to live down any other horrid magical mishap.

The genitals of Assjacket couldn't take it.

"THEY'RE ASLEEP," I WHISPERED AS I TIPTOED INTO THE GREAT ROOM and cuddled up next to Mac on the couch.

"And the cats?" he questioned warily.

"The kittens are asleep under the cribs and the obese idiots are in town playing poker with my dad."

Mac's sigh of relief made me grin. He'd been a great sport about my fat felines living in his—I mean *our* house. They were lazy and ate a ton, but they also adored Henry and Audrey and protected them vigilantly. That was their only redeeming quality in Mac's eyes, but it was a huge one so he put up with them.

"It does smell kind of minty fresh in here," I said, sniffing the air and sighing.

"Because?" Mac prompted.

"Umm… because I saw on Pinterest that toothpaste takes out grass stains."

"Seriously?"

"Not sure," I admitted. "I probably should have used Windex."

Mac closed his eyes and smiled. It was all kinds of sexy. Everything he did made my girlie parts tingle. The man could just breathe and I'd get turned on.

He thought I was crazy and he was correct. However, my intentions were good. They didn't used to be, but they were now. I had every reason to be good. Love and babies kind of did that to an uncaring materialistic witch.

"Wanna get naked and play *Goldilocks and the Three Bears*?" I asked, running my hands over his broad chest.

"Am I the Big Bad Wolf?"

"Yes."

"Do I have to wear a Granny cap and little wire-rimmed glasses?"

"Umm, no. I can't use magic so I can't conjure them up," I told him sadly. "If I use magic, you might end up with a pentagon of badoinkadoinks."

"That would be interesting," he said, pressing his forehead to mine and laughing. "I think I'm fine with one."

"You are *more* than fine with one," I assured him, crawling on top of him and straddling my beautiful man.

Pulling my cute little Prada dress over my head, I smiled coyly as Mac registered that I wasn't wearing anything underneath.

"You like?" I asked, running my hands over my body and loving the sound of his quick intake of breath.

"I love."

"Wait," I mumbled, alarmed. "I feel kind of naked." My eyes were riveted to his gorgeous chest and I couldn't raise them to meet his.

"You *are* naked," Mac pointed out with a sexy chuckle that made my girlie parts perk up substantially.

"I know," I replied with a giggle and an eye roll. "I meant I feel *weird* without magic. I can't even whip up a costume for you."

"You're not without magic," Mac said, wrapping his arms around me and pulling my body flush with his. "Everything about you is magical. You're my magic even without the spells."

"You just want to get in my pants," I told him, loving the feel of his hard body pressed against my soft.

"You're not wearing pants."

"This is true," I agreed with another giggle. "But I feel..."

"Vulnerable?"

"Yes."

Scared?"

"Yes."

"Horny?"

"Goddess, yesssssss."

"Then I think it's high time we tried out magic-less sex. You feel me?" he asked, arching his hips and making sure I knew just how horny he was.

"Kinda hard not to feel you… pun very much intended," I shot back as my hands roamed his face and my fingertips traced his full lips. "However, you're definitely overdressed for this party."

"I was hoping you might help me out with that."

Without even thinking, I raised my hands to magically remove his pants and shirt but he quickly grabbed them and pressed them to his heart.

"No can do, my beautiful witch. You're gonna have to do it the hard way… pun painfully intended," he informed me with a sexy lopsided grin that made my breath hitch.

My lady bits were singing a full scale Broadway musical and my nipples were standing at painful attention. Not to mention my heart was pounding so loudly in my chest, I was certain the noise would wake up the twins.

"Are you gonna make me do all the work?" I inquired as my green eyes locked onto his sapphire blues.

His eyes were hooded and his grin was positively carnal. "Yep."

"So damned bossy," I muttered with a giggle and a feeling of freedom. "Stand up, *werewolf*."

"My pleasure, *witch*," he shot back and stood to his full height.

I removed his clothing slowly. It was like opening the very best present in the world. His smooth skin was hot to the touch and every delectable inch of him was rock hard. Maybe magic-less sex wouldn't be so bad.

We stood inches apart and stared at each other. It was all kinds of wildly erotic and I was unsure what to do next. Normally I'd zap us into the bedroom or set us up in some kind of awesome pornographic fairy tale with full on costumes and dialogue.

Now? I was a little lost.

Fortunately Mac had an awesome sense of direction and I was happily going along for the ride.

"Oh my Goddess," I gasped out as his hands grazed my sensitive breasts and he nipped at my neck.

Returning the favor, I tried to memorize every muscle and nuance. The light sprinkling of dark hair on his chest tickled my breasts and I rubbed against him like a witch in heat. It was impossible to get close enough without crawling inside him.

"Wait, can I get knocked up?" I asked narrowing my eyes and pausing.

It wasn't that I didn't love my babies to distraction, I just wasn't in the mood to eat peanut butter-pickle-pizza with hot sauce again anytime soon.

"Not right now, baby," he whispered in my ear sending sexy chills skittering up my spine. "Do you want top or bottom?" he inquired as his strong, calloused hands gripped my ass in a hold that made my brain short circuit.

"I get to pick?" I giggled until he pressed the heel of his hand against my overheated lower region and pressed two fingers inside me. That's when my grey matter shorted out completely.

"I meant for round one. I want to taste every inch of you, but if I'm not inside of you in a matter of seconds, I think I'll die."

A ball of heat uncoiled between my legs and I was fairly sure I was going to come from his words alone. "Don't die. That would suck so bad. Besides you're on laundry duty now that I've been banned from all things domestic."

"Excellent point," he conceded as he gently pushed me down on the couch and took my mouth in a kiss that was equally as hot as sex—and trust me, sex with Mac was freakin' hot.

He tasted better than he smelled. I could have happily stayed lip-locked with him for the rest of my unnaturally long life. Of course that would be a little awkward with the kids and all. The sexy sounds coming from deep within his chest made it hard to breathe as I impatiently opened my legs to him.

"Slow or fast?" he asked, his breathing as labored as mine.

"Slow is for losers," I hissed as he entered my very willing and ready body. He was huge, hard and all mine. Life was so dang good. "Oh my Goddess, I think you got bigger. Is that badoinkadoink gonna fit?"

His decidedly masculine chuckle shot right through me and I writhed with delight beneath him. "The *badoinkadoink* will fit," he assured me and pressed deeper inside. "We were made for each other."

"Thank the Goddess for that," I said with a sigh of pleasure. My body softened and welcomed him in. "Enough chit chat. Do me."

"As you wish."

He sheathed himself inside me and I clamped around him like a vise. His lazy, sexy smile sent me into overdrive, along with a delicious feeling of fullness that straddled the line between pleasure and pain.

"Oh my hell," I gasped out and he stilled.

"You with me, baby?" he whispered in my ear.

"Forever," I whispered back, undulating my hips and feeling tingles all the way to my toes. "Pretty sure I requested that you do me. Get moving, buster."

His joyous bellow of laughter made me feel loved, safe and beautiful. How in the Goddess's green Earth did I get so lucky?

And then my werewolf *did* me. Oh my Goddess, how he *did* me. And I *did* him right back. His sinful mouth pulled into a sexy smirk as his strong body powered into mine. I was losing all rational thought and as always when we made love—had no clue where he began or I ended. This was so much more than sex. Love made sex almost unexplainable—perfect. It was life changing and just as amazing without magic.

Who knew?

Mac's breathing grew more uneven and matched my own. His eyes blazed and his fangs dropped as our lovemaking grew wilder. I cried out at the erotic invasion of my body and soul and gave back as good as I was getting. The sensitivity was almost too much to handle. My entire body trembled as he took me like the animal he was... and I freakin' loved it.

My need for him could be my undoing. My nails raked his back and my hips met every thrust with joyful abandon. I wanted to crawl inside him and stay. His face contorted, making him appear otherworldly gorgeous and the speed at which he moved became something that probably should have sent us to the Next Adventure.

A deafening roar crashed through my head and my own screams of ecstasy were sure to wake the babies. However, the mantra being whispered in my ear was clear and as exciting as any words ever spoken.

"Mine. You're mine," Mac repeated in rhythm with his thrusts.

"And you're mine," I told him on a ragged breath as my toes curled with passion.

"Come. *Now*," he demanded.

As much as I wanted to make this moment last forever I was no longer in control. This man—this wolf—owned me and I would give him whatever he wanted.

I came. Again. *Hard*.

Mac threw back his head and roared as he joined me, which sent my hooha into another violent orgasm. Colorful bursts of sparkles exploded behind my tightly closed eyes. I screamed so loudly I was sure the entirety of Assjacket would hear.

"That was..." Mac said searching for the perfect word.

"Earth shattering, amazing, wonderful and freakin' hot," I

finished his thought and laid my head on his chest. "Do you think we woke Henry and Audrey?"

We both went silent and listened. The little giggles and babbling made my heart even fuller.

"I'm gonna say yes to that," Mac said with a wide grin as he picked up my dress and slipped it over my head. "How does a family cuddle sound to you?"

Pretty sure my grin was wider than his.

"It sounds perfect. Absolutely perfect."

And it was.

It was the most magical night of my life—even without magic.

CHAPTER EIGHT

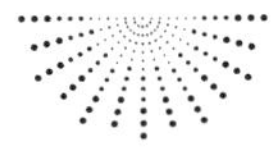

"Let's get something straight right now," Bermangoggleshitz said, barely able to keep his eyes open. "My name is Roy *Bermangoggleshitz*—not Bermangogglecrack, Bermangogglehole or Bermangoggleskank. Am I clear?"

"What about Bermangoggleturd?" I asked wondering what the heck was wrong with him. He looked exhausted.

"No."

"Bermangogglemerkin?"

"What does that even mean?" he asked, getting exasperated with me.

Goddess this might just turn out to be fun…

Sassy and I had arrived at nine AM on the dot, wearing designer combat gear from head to toe. My ensemble was hunter green to compliment my red hair and Sassy was clad in hot pink—kind of an odd choice for ass kicking lessons, but she pulled it off with her long blonde locks. We waited patiently outside my office, just in case Marge and Roy were doing something inside that would take thousands of years of therapy to remove from our brains.

Bermangoggleballs was late—fifteen minutes late and he was dragging his sorry, mostly evil butt. His eyes were squinted almost shut as if the bright morning sunlight offended him… or maybe it was the unflattering plays on his name. Whatever. If I had to be here this early so did he.

"Bermangogglemerkin is Greek," Sassy told her father. "I think it means vagina wig."

"Oh my Goddess," I shouted and slapped Sassy on the back in congratulations, sending her flying about ten feet into the bushes. "That was actually correct."

"Holy shit," she squealed with delight and skipped back over to me. "I guess I speak Greek and didn't realize it!"

"So if I'm to believe my daughter speaks *Greek*," he said looking iffy. "I then have to believe that you just called me a vagina wig?"

"Yes," I said.

"And you find this amusing?" Bermangoggleshitz asked, narrowing his one blue and one beady black eye at me.

"Yes."

Pressing his temples and clearly trying to hold his crap together, Bermangoggleshitz sighed. A small tendril of glittering black smoke wafted out of his nostril and he waved it away. "Why a vagina would need a wig is a mystery to me. You will call me *Mr. Roy*. If you so choose to mangle my name further, I will be forced to turn you into whatever horrifying moniker you bestow upon me."

Sassy raised her hand.

"Yes, Sassy?" he inquired, looking somewhat fearful.

"I'd like permission to call you Dad or sperm donor. Calling you Mr. Roy seems cold."

"Yet you're fine with calling me a toupee for feminine privates?"

Sassy looked perplexed and I realized she had no clue what her father had just said.

"Yes," she answered decisively, going with her gut and a covert nod from me.

"Dad for you," he said pointing at Sassy. "And Mr. Roy for you," he finished pointing at me.

"You have no sense of humor," I muttered.

"I'm a recovering evil warlock—a sense of humor isn't exactly in my repertoire. And I'm slightly off my game today as my *roommate* played the drums all night," he snapped.

"Marge plays the drums?" I asked with a laugh.

"Apparently she took it up last night," he hissed. "I'm working on no sleep and that makes me cranky. I'm unpleasant to begin with so I'd suggest you play by my rules or I'll change my mind about staying in the Goddess forsaken place and training your disrespectful asses."

"I'm gonna call you Rad," Sassy announced with an excited clap of her hands. "It's a combination of dad and Roy. It feels right and it's a Greek word. I speak Greek, French and English. I'm learning Chinese."

Roy nodded in confusion at his nutcase of a daughter and then eyed me expectantly.

Shit. I needed him. He knew it and I knew it. I hated losing.

"Fine, I'll call you Mr. Roy, but it will be really hard for me," I told him. "Reeeeealy hard."

"I've got it," Sassy yelled, making both of us jump. "You can call him Mr. Roy and all other words that rhyme with Mr. Roy."

I watched Roy consider Sassy's suggestion. His expression was alarmed, but he clearly couldn't think of anything that rhymed with his name that would be too offensive.

That was fine. I could come up with plenty.

He hesitated and then nodded cautiously. "That will work."

"And you won't turn me into anything?" I asked sweetly.

Again he nodded, but this time he looked wildly unsure if himself. I almost felt bad. Almost.

"Great," I said, giving him a thumbs up. "Let's get started, Blister Buttboy."

To his credit, Roy laughed—a big belly laugh. And when he laughed I was able to see a little more of his beauty. I was also secretly relieved he found my rudeness amusing. I'd hate to find out what he thought turning me into a Blister Buttboy would look like…

"Fine Helga," he said with an evil smirk. "Let's get started."

"It's Zelda," I told him, my eyebrow raised high and a smile pulling at my lips.

"That's what I said, Esmerelda."

"I see what you're doing there, Sister Soy," I said, losing the futile war with biting back my grin.

"Then you're smarter than you look," he shot back and walked out into the grassy field to start our training.

Our property was huge. It was mostly wooded with gorgeous old trees, but there were several lovely wide open fields. It was a safe haven for the shifters to shift and run without fear of being discovered by humans or more importantly human hunters.

As it was part of my job to keep the freaks of Assjacket safe, I'd warded the perimeter of our entire area against unwelcome visitors. Humans often drove through our little dump of a town, but more often than not they just kept on driving. The ward and the glamoured appearance of Main Street was very unappealing to outsiders. All magicals lived very secret lives in a public world.

The field we were to train in surrounded my office and was covered in wildflowers and long fragrant grasses. I loved looking out the windows of my office at the natural beauty that the Goddess had created. It calmed my witchy soul and made me happy.

However, I wasn't exactly happy right now. With my shitty grasp on my dark magic there was a very fine chance the beautiful field would end up a charred shit show.

"Your dad's a dick," I told Sassy with a groan as I followed the huge man who would hopefully teach me to harness my dark magic in a way that wouldn't hurt anyone or create excess genitals.

"I know," Sassy said with a happy sigh. "I just love him to bits."

~

"PRETTY SURE I HATE YOU WITH THE FIRE OF A THOUSAND SUNS," I griped as Roy made me do a hundred pushups for calling him a motherhumpin' shit monster.

"Feeling's mutual," he said flatly.

I wasn't too fond of Sassy at the moment either. She'd harnessed her dark magic in the first five minutes of training. It was so not fair. Sassy could be as daft as a bag of rocks, but she'd understood what to do immediately.

I, on the other hand, had blasted a crater the size of an SUV right in the middle of the field.

"Tell me again how you pull on your dark magic," Roy asked as he sat down on the ground next to me.

I huffed and puffed since I was only halfway through with my punishment. I really wanted to flip him off, but if I lifted my hand off the ground I would face plant for sure. My arms were shaking like leaves at the moment due to the pathetic fact that I was clearly out of shape. Not being able to use my magic was an enormous eye opener.

"I just get really pissed, let it rip and fake it," I snapped.

"Interesting," he said as he stared off into the distance.

I finished my hard labor and let my body fall to the ground. With my cheek in the dirt, I got up close and personal with my tormentor's footwear. Goddess, his boots were *freakin' awesome.*

"Are those custom?" I asked, still gulping in air.

Glancing down at me, he gave me a blank look.

"Your boots. They're rockin'. I want a pair."

His grin was contagious and as much as I wanted to turn him

into a frog with feathers and boobs, I grinned back.

"I designed them."

"Shut the fuck up, Twister Toy. You did not. You are so lying," I said, crawling closer and examining them with my trained and very materialistic eye.

Bermangoggleshitz's boots made my Doc Martens look downright wimpy. The leather was gorgeous and the design was impeccable. His boots put the shit in shit kicker.

"While lying is most definitely a favorite pastime of mine, I shit you not. I've been designing for Prada, Jimmy Choo and Manalo Blahnik for decades," he admitted with a careless shrug.

I went silent. Sassy went silent. And then we both dropped to our knees and bowed to Bermangoggleshitz.

"It can't be this easy," he muttered with a laugh. "So now I get your respect because I draw pretty shoes?"

We both nodded in unison and then went back to our prone positions.

"Up," Bermangoggleshitz directed. "If you don't piss me off, I might let you take a peek at next summer's Prada collection."

Sassy hopped to her feet and danced around. "Rad, I loved you when you were really freakin' bad and as ugly as shit on a stick. But now I actually respect you, which is weird since you're still pretty much of a semi-evil asshat with horns. But honestly, I'm happy to keep you even if you stay half butt ugly—I don't care. I mean, my mom was a total bee-otch—dumped me at an orphanage when I was tiny and left me for dead. So the fact that you want me *and* make shoes I salivate over is total icing on the motherhumpin' cake. My birthdays are so gonna rock now. And don't you worry your hideous head, I'll work very hard to learn Chinese so I can interpret for you. You seem to be a little smarter than me, but not by much—must be hereditary. And to think I married Jeeves so I wouldn't be stuck with your farked up last name and..."

"Wait." Roy waved his hand and rendered Sassy mute. "You

married a man—a kangaroo, no less—so you wouldn't be Sassy Louise Bermangoggleshitz?"

Sassy's mouth was moving a mile a minute, but no sound came out.

"Might want to undo the mute button," I suggested to Mr. Roy.

"Right."

"He's fabulous in bed. Jeeves staying power is unreal and he's huge. Just last night he…"

Quickly, Roy waved his hand again and re-muted his oversharing daughter.

"Just tell me she loves him," he said, looking pained and a bit nauseas after hearing about Sassy's sex life.

"She loves him," I promised, grinning. "Your girl was quite the wild child before Jeeves. She was more lost than I was and I was fucking lost."

"How did you two meet?" he asked still watching his daughter with curiosity.

"In the magical pokey. We were roomies," I replied, hoping he'd leave Sassy mute for the rest of our session.

"Why does that not surprise me?"

"Because you're smarter than you look," I shot back using his own line on him. "However, I *will* share that Sassy went into a meltdown when she realized Jeeves's last name was Pants."

"So Sassy *Pants* is more desirable than Sassy Bermangoggleshitz?" he asked, truly puzzled.

"I'd say it's a draw. They both suck."

He nodded absently and then glanced back at his daughter. A flash of pain and regret passed over his half beautiful- half frightening face, but he quickly masked it.

"Is it safe to let her talk?" he inquired, warily.

"No, it's never safe, but you'll get used to it."

With a brusque wave of his hand, he freed Sassy's voice. It was a risky decision, but it had to be done.

"I told him doggie style would work the best," she finished her diatribe and then heaved in a huge gulp of air as she'd clearly kept talking without breathing for at least four minutes.

"Are you done?" he asked her, trying to sound neutral.

He failed. Bermangoggleshitz sounded terrified.

"I am," she assured him. "I just wanted to say, I love you and I might hyphenate my name."

"And this is because I design shoes?" he asked, confused.

"Nooooo," Sassy said with an eye roll so large her eyes should have gotten stuck in the back of her head. "I was thinking about it before I found out you were a fucking genius. If I take on your name *too*, it moves Pants farther away from Sassy. You know... Sassy Louise *Bermangoggleshitz-Pants*. Plus all those syllables make me sound smarter. You feel me?"

As Mr. Roy was mute himself at this point, he nodded and gave his deranged offspring a weak smile.

"Okay," Sassy said, doing a few jumping jacks and landing on her ass. "Let's keep training."

"Yes," Bermangoggleshitz said, finding his voice. "Let blow some more shit up."

"Like father like daughter," I muttered, wondering how much longer we were going to have lessons this morning.

A warm wind smelling distinctly like chocolate chip cookies blew through the field and Mr. Roy screamed like a girl at a Justin Bieber concert and dove behind a pile of boulders. I just laughed and hoped the perpetrator of the wind hadn't brought her drums. The pushups had given me a serious headache. Crappy percussion would be a bad addition.

"I'm here," Marge announced as she appeared in a blast of delicious smelling smoke. "Let's get this show on the road."

"Shit," Bermangoggleshitz grumbled as he emerged from behind the rocks trying to act like he was in control and in charge.

"What's wrong, *Roy*?" Marge asked sweetly. "You look a little peaked."

"Nothing, *Marge*," he snapped. "However, I see no reason for you to participate. You have no dark magic and are therefore useless."

No one could miss Marge's swift and furious intake of breath. Sassy and I moved behind a big tree, but Roy just grinned. Apparently pissing off Marge was fun for him.

He was an idiot with a death wish—or at least someone who didn't fear lack of sleep.

"I'm your *keeper*, Roy," she informed him in a tone that clearly made him regret his impulsiveness. "Your decision, not mine."

"Yes, well," he said, trying to figure a way out. "I might have made a mistake on that."

"Too bad. So sad, Evil Boy. You make your bed and you lay in it. And for your information, magic doesn't solve everything," Marge hissed. "I know things that you don't."

"Like hideous drum playing?" he inquired rudely.

"Yes. Just wait… I brought my tuba over for tonight," she shot back with such an evil little smirk, Sassy and I laughed.

"Pushups. Now," Mr. Roy snapped at us. "Two hundred."

"My dad is a dick," Sassy whispered as she dropped to the ground and began to count.

"Yep, total and absolute dickage," I agreed as I hit the ground beside her.

"Is that Chinese?" she asked.

"No, it Penislandian."

Sassy stared at me for a long moment, slowly smiled and then nodded. "Interesting. I think I might already speak that one."

I laughed and shook my head. "Yep. Yep, I believe you do."

CHAPTER NINE

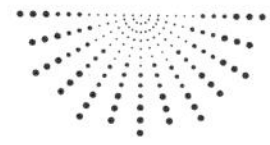

"Sassy," Roy said, completely ignoring Marge who was also studiously ignoring him.

Although, I did notice the covert longing looks he gave her when her head was turned. Bermangogglebutt had it bad for Cookie Witch. And call me crazy, but Marge's utter obnoxious rudeness might just mean she had it bad too. Only time would tell or possibly Roy would lose all his hearing due to Marge's new musical talents—or lack thereof.

"Describe dark magic," he instructed.

"In words?" Sassy asked.

"Umm… yes," Roy said.

I was pretty sure he was curious how else his daughter would explain it, but thankfully stopped himself from asking. If I had to guess, it would have been interpretive dance. She usually damaged herself when she danced—concussions, broken limbs, gaping, bloody wounds. Sassy could damage herself just walking. Dancing was a total nightmare. And since I wasn't healing anyone at the moment, it was good that Bermangoggleshitz was able to cap his curiosity. We already had enough of a shit show going on.

I'd just accidentally blasted off the side wall of my pretty office trying yet again to harness my dark voodoo.

Marge laughed with delight since it was on Roy's side of the building. Lister Coy simply grunted and repaired it with an eye roll and a wave of his hand.

"Well," Sassy said, wrinkling her nose and thinking hard.

I was surprised smoke didn't come out of her ears.

"For me, dark magic is Cupid's tears, witch veins, sirens' screams and fairy laughter."

Marge stared at Sassy in shock. My mouth hung open in awe and confusion. But Bermangoggleshitz simply smiled and patted his daughter's head.

"Did I get it right?" she asked with wide eyes.

"Everyone's answer is unique to its owner, my child," he said with a shrug. "For me, it's the Devil's laugh, black cats, Mermaid tails, and flower petals."

Sassy nodded in understanding. "I like that."

"Wait a motherhumpin' minute. What in the Goddess's thong are you people blabbering about?" I demanded.

Roy turned his attention to me. "What do you think dark magic is?"

"A fucking pain in my ass," I snapped. "It produces multiple weenies and craters in the field—not to mention it blows off the sides of office buildings."

"And *that's* your problem," he said. "Learn to love what is yours. If you hate it, it will hate you back."

"Look dude, I just learned to love myself. And let me tell you something, that was not easy—at all. So if you're telling me I have to learn to love evil on top of all the other shit I'm supposed to love, you're a bigger crusty knob tyrant than I thought you were."

With a snarl and a shake of his head, Bermangoggleshitz crossed over to me. I shrank back and wished for the ten millionth time I had a fucking filter. He'd made me do pushups for calling him a shit monster. I was probably going to have to run a freakin' marathon for this one.

"Don't think," he instructed harshly. "Describe dark magic. NOW."

"Vampire bites, nightmares, Demons fire, and pentagons," I shouted and then shuddered.

"Pentagons?" he questioned.

"Five penises," Sassy clarified. "She gave Roger five badoinkadoinks. I likened it to a pentagon of penii."

"They're connected?" Bermangoggleshitz asked, aghast.

Little sparks of pissed off black magic bounced off of me and singed the grass. "No," I shouted and stomped my foot creating another unfortunate large hole in the ground. "And thank the Goddess for that small, puny favor—penis pun intended. Roger would have had a very difficult time taking a leak if they were. However, if you keep being such a large gaping douche canoe asscracker, I might have a go at yours and see if I can make it happen again. You feel me, Fever Blister Toy?"

"Calm down, Zelda," Marge said in a no-nonsense tone. "We will not be reshaping any male appendages on purpose. It's bad karma. I understand what Roy means, and if you stop and think for a moment, you will as well."

Goddess, I hated it when everyone was right and I was wrong. It was happening far too often lately for my liking.

"Can I just pretend I love it?" I asked, searching really hard to find a quick fix.

"No," Roy said. "It will know."

"How do you love evil?" I snapped. "That seems more like bad karma than a pants-full of peens."

Roy jerked forward to protect his package and gave me a stern look that scared the hell out of me. It was easy to forget how powerful the warlock was since he was trying to leave his villainous ways behind. But only a fool would underestimate him. I was many things, but I wasn't a fool.

"You have to find it within," he growled. "I can't do that for you."

"Then what good are you?" I demanded, at a loss for anything to do but yell at him. "I can't exactly do my job if I'm a genital risk."

That one left him speechless. It kind of left me speechless too.

I was worthless if I couldn't protect and heal my ragtag tribe of dumbasses. I'd finally found a home, happiness, a purpose… and love. And now I was screwing all of it up because I had no clue how to get lovey-dovey with the dark magic I didn't want in the first place.

"I'm not gonna let her win," I muttered, walking about a fifty yards away from Roy, Marge and Sassy. If I was going to try again, I needed room.

"You're not going to let who win?" Marge asked.

I glanced back at her and frowned. "My mother. She didn't love me, which almost derailed my happiness. Now I have her dark magic and it's on its way to derailing me again."

"If you give your mother that much power over you, then your failure is your own fault," Marge said flatly, with an odd expression on her face I couldn't quite read.

She really needed to shut her cakehole. Cookie Witch had no clue what my mother had been like or what I'd had to do to end her reign of terror. Marge could spout witchy wisdom all day, but until she could tell me she'd punched her fist into her mother's chest to remove her magic and got stuck with uncontrollable dark magic that gave her therapist five peens, I didn't want to hear it. Besides, I was pretty sure she and her sister Baba Yaga had been hatched—not born.

"Yep," I snapped with an eye roll. "You didn't have my mother."

"And you didn't have mine," she shot back.

If we were going to get into a *who had the worst mom contest*, I was going to win. I was sure of it.

"She hated me," I said.

"Ditto," Marge shot back. "Mine used Carol and me horribly."

"Ditto," I snapped. "She turned my father into a cat when he found out about me and tried to find me."

"I have no clue who my father was," Marge said. "My egg donor was a horridly unhappy woman and took great pleasure in making sure Carol and I were miserable."

"Fine. It's a tie," Bermangoggleshitz said, ending the one-upping. "I can confirm Marge's mother was hideous. However, it's a choice," Bermangoggleshitz said, clearly not up for listening to a pity party about our mommy issues. "*Your choice*. Blame is as useless as a one-legged warlock in an ass kicking contest."

"Good one, Rad," Sassy congratulated her father who looked pleased with her approval.

I just rolled my eyes. "Why was it so easy for Sassy?"

Sassy stepped forward and took her father's hand. "I was born with dark magic, Zelda. It's always been part of me. Pretty sure that's why I enjoy blowing up buildings so much. But I've had my whole life to deal with it. I can safely say I haven't always been successful, which is why I ended up in the pokey."

"Dating Baba Yaga's former boyfriend didn't help either," I reminded her with a small grin.

"This is true," Sassy said with a giggle. "That whiney warlock was such a wad. Anyhoo, it really wasn't until I found you... and then Jeeves... that I truly had a handle on it. Now whenever I want to blow the shit out of something, I just blow the shit out of Jeeves."

There was a long, puzzled and uncomfortable silence while everyone let Sassy's words sink in. Roy studied the ground at his feet as if was the most interesting thing he'd ever seen and Marge's hand flew to her mouth. She was either trying not to laugh or gasp.

"Did she just say what I think she said?" Bermangoggleshitz asked, paling considerably.

"Yes. Yes she did," Marge answered him with a pained laugh.

"Intellectually, I understand," I conceded, deciding to ignore that Sassy just announced that she funneled her need to detonate buildings into giving her kangaroo husband blowjobs. "However, it took therapy with Roger—the rabbit I gifted with multiple dongs —and doing the musical of *Mommie Dearest* to make me learn how to love myself. Don't know what it's gonna take to make me love my dark doodoo."

"Voodoo," Sassy corrected me.

"I like doodoo better."

"Is that Chinese?"

"No, it's Profanican."

"Got it," Sassy said with a delighted laugh. "I'm fluent in that fucking shit."

"I understood very little of that exchange," Bermangoggleshitz whispered, running his hands through his hair and probably regretting taking us on. "Are you saying you need therapy and a *Joan Crawford musical* to get a grip on your power?"

"I'm saying I don't know," I replied, feeling defeated. "I just don't know."

"Wait," Roy said, still stuck on what I'd revealed to him only moments ago. "*Mommie Dearest* is a musical?"

"Yep. Huge no more wire hangers number," I told him.

"That's..." He was at a loss for words.

As anyone should be when they learned the stupefying news of what Assjackians considered art.

"Wrong," I finished for him.

"On so many levels," Marge added with a laugh. "I so wish I'd seen that."

"No you don't," I told her grinning. "It was all kinds of awful and cringey."

"I disagree," Sassy cut in. "I was fabulous as Christina even though Bob the beaver sucked ass as Christopher. I think if he'd plucked his unibrow the production would have been much better. Also I think a huge mistake was made when Fabio took Jeeves out of the Christopher role. I thought the underlying sexual tension between Christopher and Christina made the musical have bigger, hairier balls."

"Aren't they brother and sister?" Bermangoggleshitz choked out with a horrified wince.

"*Adopted* brother and sister," Sassy corrected him.

Again Sassy caused shocked silence. She was so good at that.

Marge clapped her hands and conjured up three wooden chairs and rope. "Well, Zelda, while you figure out how to love the darkness, I'm going to teach you two how to defend yourselves without magic. And Sassy dear, this will work better if you don't speak."

"Roger that," Sassy said with a nod and a clueless thumbs up.

"You're going to have them beat on each other with chairs?" Roy inquired with a sarcastic snort.

"No, we're going to beat on you with chairs."

"Seriously?" he asked, not liking the direction of what was supposed to be his teaching lesson.

"Very," Marge replied with an innocent smile. "Certainly you're not afraid of three witches not using their magic."

"Should I be?" he asked warily.

"Yes. Very."

~

"WHY AM I TIED TO A CHAIR?" I ASKED, UNABLE TO MOVE MUCH MORE than my mouth and feet.

"It ensures you can't use your hands to perform magic," Marge said as she checked the knots she'd tied on both Sassy and me.

"Okay," I said with an eye roll. I didn't need my hands to perform a spell. I just needed my mouth. Marge knew this, but she did have a point. Waving my hand and fixing something with enchantment was second nature. "Why aren't you tied to a chair?"

"Because I'm teaching you."

"As shocking as it may sound, I have to agree with Zelda on this one," Roy chimed in with an evil little smirk on his face. "I'd be happy to tie you to the chair and gag you while I'm at it."

With a wiggle of her nose, Marge gagged Roy with a huge wad of goopy pink frosting. It was perfect since he couldn't remove the gag. He had to eat it. That would take at least ten minutes. I really did love Marge's style.

"You can move your legs below the knee," Marge pointed out.

"Yep," Sassy said, leaning forward and kind of standing up only to land flat on her face.

Quickly Roy righted his daughter as he worked his way through the frosting. The vicious glare he gave Marge would have been terrifying if half of his face wasn't covered in the bubblegum pink sugary confection.

"Zelda, if I told you to take Roy down right now what would you do?" Marge asked.

"Umm… laugh at you?" I answered.

"Nope," she said with a chuckle as she waved her hand and magically tied herself to her own chair. "Watch. Attack me, Roy."

"Really, *Marge*?" Roy questioned sarcastically, finally done eating his frosting gag. "You can't be serious."

"Oh, but I am, *Roy*," she replied calmly. "Come at me. No magic this time."

"Sounds kinky," he replied with a grin, making Marge blush with fury.

"Your daughter is present," she snapped primly and shot him a glare that made his smirk disappear fast. "You will come at me as if I was your prisoner."

"If you were tied up, I wouldn't need to attack you," he pointed out logically.

"This is true," she said, frowning and agreeing with him. "I guess we can't do this. Can you please come untie me?"

What was happening here? Was Cookie Witch that much off her game? All of this felt like a massive waste of time at this point.

Bermangoggleballs couldn't tell me how to love my evil parts and Marge had tied all of us to chairs for apparently no reason.

Freakin' awesome.

And what happened next proved yet again how wrong I could be...

As Bermangoggleshitz approached Marge with a delighted yet obnoxiously condescending expression on his face, Marge leaned forward on the front right leg of her chair. It all happened so freakin' fast I wasn't sure I even caught all her moves.

Spinning on the front leg of her chair, she knocked the feet from under the shocked warlock who landed on his back with a thud while spewing a string of swear words that I needed to write down for future use. It was awesome, but Cookie Witch wasn't done.

As her back was now facing the prone and confused Bermangoggleshitz, she leaned forward and sprang off her feet, throwing her body and the chair backwards. She rose up about four feet before she landed with a sickening crunch on top of Roy.

Roy then of course let out another string of profanity that was even better than his first. It did come out a bit garbled since Marge had head-butted him upon her landing and clearly broken his nose.

What should have been the end wasn't...

Marge twisted like some ninja on speed and landed back on the bleeding Bermangoggleshitz with her knee planted firmly in his crotch. This time his cussfest came out ten pitches higher than the last two, but it was no less colorful.

Bermangoggleshitz could cuss me under the table and that was no small feat.

"And *that* was for trying to steal the secret recipe and screwing around on me for hundreds of years," she hissed, nose to bloody nose with the most badass warlock I'd ever come across.

"Holy shit," Sassy said. "That was impressive, but I kind of feel sorry for my Rad."

"No, no," he said, lifting Marge off of him and gently setting her chair on the ground. "I'm afraid I deserved that and more. Marge has every right to pay me back. I welcome it."

Instead of looking victorious, Marge looked aghast at what she had just done. Her lovely chin dropped to her chest and she appeared to be crying. What in the ever lovin' hey hey was going on here?

"I'm sorry Roy," she mumbled as she wiggled her nose and freed all of us from our ropes. "That was uncalled for."

"But it worked," Sassy pointed out thoughtfully as she removed her combat jacket and started mopping the blood from her father's face. "You took him down without magic."

"Yes, but he didn't use any magic to retaliate," I argued. "This could have gone really wrong if it was real."

"Possibly," Roy said. "However, with Marge tied up, I didn't see it coming. Surprise was the element. Split seconds can make the difference between life and death. Not that I particularly enjoyed that exhibition, Marge was correct to show you how it could be done."

"Nevertheless, it was a bit excessive," Marge admitted, still unable to make eye contact with any of us. "Being mean and vengeful doesn't feel good."

"My point exactly," I said so loudly I startled myself. "Evil is mean. It doesn't feel good. How in the Goddess's booty shorts am I supposed to love it?"

"Let's tackle that tomorrow," Roy said with a grimace smile, still trying to stem the blood pouring from his nose. "I do believe I need to pay a visit to Fabio for a healing."

"Zelda could give it a try," Sassy volunteered.

Jackknifing forward in a universally male protective stance, he shook his head. "Umm… not today. I've had all the disfigurement I'd like for now."

"You're smarter than you look," I said with a laugh.

"So I've been told," he replied dryly. "Shall we go?"

"Yep," Sassy said, wrapping her arms around her father's waist and walking him off the field.

"Are you coming?" I asked, looking back at Cookie Witch who stood frozen in her spot.

"No, dear. I have some thinking to do. You go ahead. I'll see you later."

Marge graced me with a distracted smile and then disappeared in a cloud of gingerbread scented wind.

This was a *weird* day and I had a *weirder* feeling it would only get more bizarre.

CHAPTER TEN

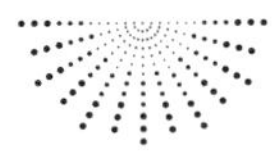

Bermangogglebloodynose was seated on my couch. Sassy had found some plastic for him to sit on so he wouldn't destroy my beautiful sofa. Fabio circled him, looking at the warlock from all angles. Roy wasn't a happy camper at the moment. Fabio was enjoying himself a bit too much for Roy's pleasure.

"Explain to me again how this happened," Fabio asked as he continued examine Bermangoggleshitz's broken nose with amusement.

"Marge kicked his ass while tied to a chair, using no magic at all," Sassy said.

"And you did *nothing*?" Fabio asked Roy.

"Define nothing," Roy said.

"I meant nothing to deserve *this*." Fabio gestured to the bloody mess that doubled as Bermangoggleshitz's face.

Thankfully Fabio had been at Mac's and my house when we'd arrived. He was playing with the twins—or more likely teaching them something wildly illegal. At least the cats weren't here to add to the shit show. Mac was in town dealing with some inebriated raccoon Shifters who thought peeing a huge heart on Main Street in broad daylight was an outstanding idea.

Fabdudio had taken one look at Roy and burst into laughter. Roy wasn't too amused, but as he needed Fabio to heal him, he simply grunted and flipped my father off.

"Well," Roy said with a very small grim smile pulling at his lips. "If you want to add up past offenses, I'd be at a loss as how to answer that."

"Ahhh." Fabio nodded and chuckled. "Then my guess would be that this is the tip of the iceberg. You should probably watch your back… or your crotch, if you want to keep it intact."

"She nailed that too," Sassy volunteered.

"I didn't see it coming," Roy admitted sheepishly. "And I wouldn't have done anything even if I had. I believe that kicking my ass or lodging my testicles in my throat is on Marge's bucket list."

"I think she likes him," I said, bouncing Henry and Audrey on my knees and kissing their adorable chubby faces. "Marge has an odd and rather violent way of showing it, but she did live in a wrinkle by herself for hundreds of years. Her people skills could use some work."

"You think I have a chance?" Bermangoggleshitz asked doubtfully.

"Not the way you're working it at the moment," I replied, scrunching my nose and giving him a thumbs down on his wooing ability.

"Look, Rad," Sassy said taking Henry into her arms and cuddling him. "Ol' Cookie Witch doesn't really like idiots all that much. I'm the exception since I have to take over her suck ass job eventually. You are kind of the King of Idiots. You feel me?"

"Umm…" Roy always seemed to be at a loss where conversing with his spawn was concerned. He definitely wasn't the only one. We were just more used to Sassy's convoluted train of thought.

"So I say you play hard to get," she went on oblivious to her father's bewilderment. "You know... start dating a few gals in town, walk around shirtless, flex a lot, take a shower with the door open. Make Marge see what she's missing."

"Umm... nope." I shot that one down immediately. "First off, that's a shitty idea. If you were listening to Marge's list of Bermangoggledumbass's transgressions, you'd recall she kneed his nuts because he cheated on her—which is very, very bad in case you didn't know," I told an embarrassed Bermangoggleshitz. "Second off, even though you're improving in the looks department, you're still pretty much half-buttass ugly. I think you're gonna just have to go with your gut. What do you usually do to get a gal?"

"Umm..." Again Roy was at a loss.

"Dude," I said with an eye roll. "You can't tell me you haven't dated since you screwed over Marge. That had to be hundreds of years ago."

"Define *date*," he requested, truly puzzled.

Blowing out a long put upon sigh, I eyed the enormous warlock with the bloody broken nose. What I was about to offer was redonkulous, but... if I couldn't heal with magic, maybe I could heal in other ways.

"How about this..." I said slowly, wondering if I had gone insane. No wait. I was completely insane and about to prove it. Whatever. It felt right. "I'll help you not be such a jackwad in the Marge department and you lay off the pushups when you train me."

Roy stood and his eyes narrowed as he considered my offer. He appeared hopeful and terrified at the same time. He was smarter than he looked.

"Are those your *only* terms?" he inquired with a raised brow.

"Of course not," I answered with a laugh. "I don't have to call you Mr. Roy and you design a pair of boots similar to yours for me."

"And me," Sassy chimed in.

"And Sassy," I amended.

"Roy designs shoes?" Fabio asked, surprised.

"For Prada, Jimmy Choo and Manalo Blahnik," I told my dad.

Without missing a single beat, Fabio was on it. "I'd like a pair in black."

Shaking his head, Roy chuckled. "Fine. Boots all around. You really think you can help me?"

"No clue, but I can certainly do better than you're doing right now."

"Zelda has a point, Rad," Sassy said. "Your skills suck."

"Fine. I accept," Roy said, still looking petrified.

"Well, good luck to you," Fabio told him. "However, I believe we should take care of that nose before you let Zelda become your Cyrano De Bergerac."

"It's Houston," Sassy corrected Fabio. "Zelda changed her name to Houston, not Cerano De Buttcrack."

"Right," Fabio said, knowing far better than to try to correct Sassy or explain what he'd meant. "Sit down, Roy."

Roy sat.

Fabio healed.

Kind of…

It was a known fact that female witch healers were far stronger than male warlock healers. I'd just never seen proof until now.

"Umm… Fabdudio," I said, wincing as he hopped around the room groaning in pain and frantically searching for something to stem the blood now pouring from his own nose.

Bermangoggleshitz was completely fine—nose as good as new. My dad? Not so much.

"Is that supposed to happen?" Roy asked, shocked.

"No," I replied, grabbing a clean burb cloth and shoving it into my dad's hands. "What gives?"

"Not sure," Fabio said as confused as Roy. "I normally take on the pain of what I heal—not the actual injury. This is odd."

"Sit down and put your head back," Sassy instructed. "I'm gonna go find some fucking Windex."

"Do *not* let her use Windex on my face," Fabio begged as he shoved the edges of the burb cloth up each nostril.

"It worked in *My Big Fat Greek Wedding*," Roy pointed out.

"Oh my Goddess," I grumbled. "She is so your daughter."

While I pondered what in the ever-loving hell to do, Sassy arrived with the Windex, which my father promptly conjured into a Birkin bag. Sassy was so taken with the purse, she forgot all about spraying my dad's face with window cleaner.

"I'm no good at this," Fabio said. "We could be in big trouble here if someone gets seriously injured."

"Buwsit Crapass," Henry said, standing up on his chunky baby legs and pointing his finger at his defeated grandfather.

"Buzzhit Kapass," Audrey joined in.

She, too pointed at Fabio. Both of my children were grinning from ear to ear and I let my head fall in defeat. I was fairly sure their first words were definitely profane.

It was now official. I sucked ass as a mom.

"What did they say?" Bermangoggleshitz asked.

"I speak baby," Sassy announced. "They said, 'bullshit I crapped my pants' or they might have said, '*Krampas* is a bullshit movie' or most likely they said, 'bullshit Grandpa'. The only word I'm sure of is bullshit."

Before I could cry or admonish my gorgeous babies for swearing, they crawled over to Fabio and onto his lap. Gently touching his face and whispering nonsensical loving words they closed their eyes and hummed.

The atmosphere of the room went from normal to magical in a split second. Tiny golden sparks danced around my children's red curls like miniature sparkling halos. Their giggles produced more sparkles in pinks, teals and silver. Fabio was covered from head to toe in an enchantment like I'd never witnessed. As the magic drifted away, Fabio sighed with contented relief.

"Busssit Crapass," Audrey said, planting a wet kiss on Fabio's perfectly healed nose.

"I'm thinking they just named you Crapass," Sassy said with a laugh.

"They can call me whatever they want," Fabio said, cuddling my children close and showering them with kisses. "Anything their little hearts desire and I will answer to it."

"My Goddess," Bermangoggleshitz gasped out. "They shift and heal? What else can they do?"

My head whipped around so fast, Roy jumped back to avoid ending up crispy. Black sparks flew from my fingertips and I was this close to blasting Roy to the Next Adventure.

"You. Saw. Nothing," I ground out through clenched teeth. "Do you feel me? I don't care how powerful you are or how semi-evil, I will take you to hell and drop you off if you tell anyone about my children."

Bermangoggleshitz observed me with a small smile playing on his lips. "Do you love your dark magic right now?"

His question threw me.

"I love that I could end you if you wanted to harm my children," I growled.

"So you do love it?" he pressed.

Inhaling deeply through my nose, I got a handle on my fury. The black magic receded and I stared him right in the eye. "Yes, I love it right now."

"Do you think fate wanted you to have this particular gift to protect what is yours?" Bermangoggleshitz asked.

"Fate is as crazy as a motherhumpin' loon. And the answer is... *I don't know,*" I snapped, getting more confused. "So fine... maybe I can learn to love my dark side, but I still don't know how to control it."

"I'd say you're doing pretty good, Houston," Sassy chimed in. "Rad, do you have more than one badoinkadoink at the moment?"

Fabio's bark of laughter and Roy's gasp of horror would have been hilarious if all of this wasn't so farked up.

Quickly turning his back to us, Bermangoggleshitz checked his man bits and sighed dramatically in relief. "Only one," he said.

"See?" Sassy squealed, grabbing me and hugging me tight. "You were furious at my Rad, but you didn't multiply his knob even though your dark magic was on full display. You've so got this, dude."

"That's a bit premature—no genital pun intended," Roy said. "But we've made progress. And Zelda, you have my word that I will never reveal anything about your children."

"Your word means nothing to me," I told him flatly. "You come with a really bad track record."

Bermangoggleshitz bowed his head in shame and understanding. "What can I do to assure you?"

I didn't have to think at all. The most binding oath we had was Witches Honor—or in a male's case—Warlock's Honor. However, I had a little extra twist.

"You will swear on your honor, promising the Goddess to give up all your power and become human if you should break your vow."

Fabio's sharp intake of breath and Sassy's gasp made me very aware of the gauntlet I'd just thrown down, but I stood by it. I would die for my children and no one was going to harm them on my clock.

"I will swear," Bermangoggleshitz said without a beat of hesitation.

His immediate response surprised me, but a lot of things about Bermangoggleshitz were beginning to surprise me.

"Let's do this outside," Fabio suggested. "The Goddess will most certainly have something to add to the conversation and I'd think lightning in the house wouldn't go over too well with Mac."

"Excellent idea," Bermangoggleshitz concurred as he walked to the front door and opened it.

"You're probably gonna get an ass zapping from the Goddess. I get one at least once a week and I'm way better behaved than you are," Sassy said, skipping out of the house after her father.

Fabio stood up with a baby in each arm. "You're a good mother, my child."

"Their first word was bullshit. That's not really great parenting," I said, mortified. "Don't know how I'm gonna explain that one to Mac."

Fabio laughed and planted a kiss on the top of my head. "Mac will be fine. He loves you *and* your potty mouth. I promise. You really ready to force Bermangoggleshitz's hand?"

"Yep. That doesn't faze me at all. Henry and Audrey will always come first."

"As I said... you are a wonderful mother."

"You're actually a pretty good dad and Crapass, too," I shot back.

"Crapass," Henry and Audrey sang as we walked out the front door together.

I suppose his name could have been worse, but I couldn't for the life of me figure out how.

CHAPTER ELEVEN

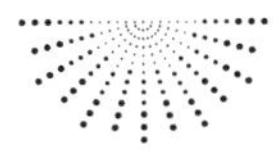

"How do we do this?" Bermangoggleshitz asked, unsure of the procedure. "I'm not exactly on good terms with the Goddess at the moment."

The day was winding down and the sun sat low and blazing orange on the horizon. A gentle breeze blew through the long grasses surrounding our property. The trees rustled and the birds sang. I sighed and smiled. The Goddess had created such a beautiful world.

"You promise on Warlock's Honor and we see what she does," I told him. "Sit down and feel the earth beneath you. You need to get back in touch with your earth magic, dude. It misses you."

He looked at me strangely but followed my directions. "Pretty sure it doesn't like me," Roy muttered as his hands sunk into the grass and he breathed in a huge cleansing breath.

"Feels good, doesn't it?" I asked, feeling superior to him for once. He might have the edge on dark magic, but I was pretty dang good at the light stuff.

Bermangoggleshitz nodded and closed his eyes. "Goddess, if you are listening to an old man with much to regret, I have something to say."

The wind stopped and the birds went silent. The sun shimmered so brightly that I had to shield my eyes. Holy crap on a sharp stick, this was bizarre. Fabdudio was definitely right to take this potential shit storm outside.

The air sizzled with enchantment and purple sparks began to rain down from the sky. Bermangoggleshitz stood slowly and stared in wonder. He lifted his hands to catch the glimmering magic as a child would to catch the first few flakes of winter's earliest snowstorm.

His voice started in a whisper and then grew stronger as he spoke.

"I swear on Warlock's Honor, to never reveal my knowledge of Henry or Audrey. If I break my oath, I forfeit my magic and will take on a human life. I choose to go further and pledge to protect the children from the darkness and when the time comes, I shall teach them how to wield their own dark magic. Hear me, Goddess... and give an undeserving man your blessing."

A strong gust of rain scented wind blew through the yard knocking Sassy, Roy, Fabio and me to the ground, but not my babies. The current gently lifted them and they floated above us with babbling joy. The Goddess had wrapped them in her loving grace and cuddled them with nature.

Bursts of blissful magic surrounded Henry and Audrey and they swatted at it gleefully. I knew I wasn't quite right in the head, but I would swear the wind was laughing with delight.

Then the wind spoke.

And I realized as crazy as I was, I wasn't crazy at all. The Goddess created nature and she communicated through it as well. I'd just never heard her so clearly—or maybe I hadn't listened hard enough. The words were melodic and airy. I'd honestly never known the Goddess to speak. I'd always taken the wrath of her anger for my impertinence right on my ass. She could say a whole freakin' hell of a lot with a well-placed bolt of magic.

But this was surreal. My heart felt full and tears filled my eyes.

"I accept your oath and shall forever hold you to your promise, Roy Bermangoggleshitz. You have much to atone for and you shall begin now."

And with a crack of silver blue lightning that landed squarely on Bermangoggleshitz's ass, the world went right back to normal. The birds resumed singing and the trees continued to rustle and sway.

My babies floated back down and crawled straight to Bermangoggleshitz who was rolling in the grass to extinguish the fire on his ass. His language was all sorts of appalling, but I really couldn't blame him. Those ass cracks of lightning hurt like a motherhumper.

"Watch your mouth, Rad," Sassy admonished her father. "Henry and Audrey already say bullshit, they don't need to learn any more bad words from you."

Bermangoggleshitz grunted his agreement and lay on the ground in exhaustion. He'd been nailed by a chair and blasted by the Goddess. Not to mention he'd had no sleep due to Marge's desire to become the next Ringo Starr.

"Houston, do you mind if I use a little magic and put out my Rad's ass fire?"

"Be my guest," I told her, getting unfortunately used to her calling me by the name of a city. "You have a handle on your dark magic. You're not a genital risk."

"Thanks, dude," Sassy said as she waved her hand and created a brief mini rain shower over her dad's smoldering butt."

"Look at me, Roy," Fabio said, squatting down next to him and helping him to a seated position. "Goddess, I can't believe it."

"Believe what?" I asked, running over.

"Holy schnikes!" Sassy yelled, gaping at her dad. "Rad, you're prettier. I mean you've still got some butt ass ugly going, but you're getting pretty hot."

And she was correct. Bermangoggleshitz was going from the Beast to Beauty. Not completely. He still had horns. I did wonder if he would ever truly go back to his original visage, but… he was getting closer.

"Dude," I said with a grin. "Your good is showing."

"Yes, well… being good is extremely painful and tiring," he said with a grimace as he got to his feet.

"Are you hungry?" Sassy asked her dad.

"Are you offering to cook for me?"

"Goddess no!" she shouted. "You'd die of food poisoning. However, Jeeves is cooking at the Assjacket Diner tonight and I'd like to treat my semi-heinous dad to a delicious meal."

"I could go for that as well," Fabio said. "Shall we take my car?"

"How about we take our brooms?" Sassy suggested.

Fabio and Bermangoggleshitz gaped at her in horrified shock.

"Sassy," I said with an eye roll and a laugh. "Broomsticks and testicles are not friends. Your dad and mine have been through enough today and I'm quite sure Fabdudio doesn't want to heal Roy's nuts or his own. You feel me?"

"I could put cushioned seats on the brooms," she argued her case.

"No," Bermangoggleshitz said firmly. "But thank you, darling. And umm… you do realize we don't need brooms to fly, right?"

"I know that," she said with a giggle. "I just think it's so cool and it's awfully terrifying to see a bunch of witches flying into town on bushy sticks."

Fabio and Bermangoggleshitz exchanged looks and then shrugged. Sassy took that as a yes and conjured up three seated brooms before they could change their minds.

"You want one Zelda? I could make a three seater for you and the kids."

"No. Never. Definitely not. I'm going to wait for Mac to get home and we'll meet you flying idiots at the diner."

"Good plan," Sassy yelled as she hopped on her broom and made ridiculous revving noises with her mouth.

I stood and watched the three of them blast into the air. Bermangoggleshitz screamed and ended up riding upside down—something I was sadly familiar with. Fabio faired only slightly better as he listed to the right and pretty much won the screaming contest. For two of the most powerful warlocks in existence, they were pretty wimpy.

"Crapass," Audrey yelled with delight as she pointed to the sky.

"Buwsit," Henry added with a belly laugh.

Scooping the little giggle monsters up into my arm, I had to agree with my son. Riding a broom was total bullshit. I just hoped Roy and Fabio had more graceful landings than I'd had.

Somehow, I doubted it. The thought made me grin.

"Let's get you guys changed and wait for daddy. Okay?"

"Buzzshit," they shouted happily.

Oh well, I suppose it was good that asshat or motherfucker or crusty butt-whacker hadn't been their first word. Not that bullshit was great, but everything could always be worse.

CHAPTER TWELVE

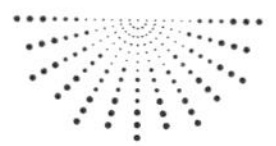

"I'm not exactly the kind of warlock one wants to bring home to their mother," Bermangoggleshitz pointed out, digging into the fried chicken and mashed potatoes Jeeves had made.

The diner was full of happy Shifters eating the delicious food Jeeves had cooked. The Assjacket Diner was one of my favorite places in town. It was full of charming décor and delicious aromas. The tables were all a dark heavy wood covered in charming Shabby Chic-ish tablecloths and kitschy mismatched napkins. Floral teacups and saucers like a grandma should have sat atop the tables and screamed for the Shifters to drink from them with an extended pinkie. It was fabulous. Wanda and DeeDee, the owners, were milling around refreshing iced teas and tempting people with their melt in your mouth desserts.

Thankfully Fabio had been correct about the first word debacle. Mac laughed when I'd told him what our babies had said. However, he'd laughed so hard I thought he might choke when I revealed Fabio's new name. I had a feeling he'd be referring to my dad as Crapass from now on. That should go over outstandingly.

Mac and my dad had a mostly polite truce as my dad was still a little put out that I'd mated with a werewolf instead of a warlock.

"Well, since Marge and Baba Yomamma don't have a mother anymore, you should be fine," I said, cutting up chicken into tiny pieces for Henry and Audrey. My babies were covered in mashed potatoes and digging into the green beans like they were candy. They were fabulous eaters—just like their momma.

I didn't realize Fabdudio, Mac and Roy were staring at me in shock, until I noticed the entire table was silent.

"What?"

"They still have a mother," Fabio said with a shudder.

"I call bullpoop on that. Marge did say her mom was a gaping jackhole of massive proportions, but she talked about her in past tense. Anyhoo, I'm still not sold that they actually had a mom at all. I'm positive they were hatched by aliens who then sold them because they were such nightmares."

"While that's an interesting theory, it's not quite right, babe," Mac said, passing me the hot sauce that I loved to put on all my food.

"Seriously? I was sure I was right," I said with a laugh, handing Audrey back the sippy cup that she'd just lobbed at her brother.

"I always thought they were created by the Goddess—kind of like Frankenstein," Sassy announced. "And that Baba Yaga's bobble-headed warlock posse were all pooped out by aliens in an explosion of diarrhea."

"I like that story better," I told her with a high five.

"Buzzit," Henry yelled, raising his little fists full of green beans in the air.

"Doooraaa!" Audrey squealed and giggled as she hurled her mashed potato covered sippy cup at Crapass.

Fabio paled and caught the cup as he leaned into Audrey. "How do you know that?" he asked my daughter in a strangled whisper.

"Know what?" I asked, alarmed. "What's a Doooraaa?"

"Endora," Bermangoggleshitz whispered in a shaky voice.

"Who is Endora?" I demanded. I wasn't in the mood to play the guessing game and I wasn't into anyone being cryptic at the moment. I had green beans in my hair and mashed potatoes on my shirt. That was all the fun and games I was up for.

"Endora is Baba Yaga and Marge's mother," Mac explained, paling just like my father had.

My laugh was loud and all three men glanced around the diner in fear. "Her name is Endora? Like the mom in *Bewitched?*"

"*Exactly* like the mom in *Bewitched,*" Bermangoggleshitz whispered, still looking around warily.

"*Painfully* like the mother in *Bewitched,*" Fabio added, following Roy's lead and scanning the diner.

"She *is* the mother from *Bewitched,*" Mac said with a small shudder.

"Hold the fuck up," Sassy said with a laugh. "That was a freakin' TV show and the mom was an actress."

"Sassy, the word fuck is now replaced with fark," I told her, nodding at the listening babies. "We have repeaters."

"My bad," Sassy apologized. "I meant hold the fark up. That was a farkin' TV show and the mom was a motherfarkin' actress. Better?"

"Much," I replied with an eye roll. "The joke is a little funny, guys. But it's not that funny."

"Not a joke," Fabio said. "Endora wanted to be a star so she took the stage name Agnes Moorehead and auditioned for *Bewitched*. The original script had named the matriarch, Glinda, but Endora did a little voodoo and had the name changed."

"You're shitting me," I said. I'd done some crazy things, but that was bizarre.

"I shit you not," Fabio said. "She glamoured herself to age and then eventually had to let Agnes die so no one would be the wiser."

"So she's alive?" Sassy asked.

Bermangoggleshitz nodded gravely. "Endora is definitely alive."

This was some seriously unwelcome news if the reactions of my father, Roy and Mac were anything to go by. Not to mention Marge's horrible earlier description of her. "And how does Audrey know about her?"

"My guess is that Endora has paid the children a visit or two," Fabio whispered.

"How in the Goddesses jockstrap did a witch show up here in Assjacket and I didn't know about it?" I demanded.

I'd warded the entire town and Mac was able to sense foreign magic in his kingdom. There was no way a witch got in here without our knowledge.

"She's older than dirt," Bermangoggleshitz said. "She can do things no one else can."

"Like kidnap my children?" I snapped as glittering black zaps of magic exploded from my fingertips and set the table on fire.

Waving her chubby little hands, Audrey created a rainstorm above our table and Henry—not to be outdone by his sister—added a few claps of thunder.

Amazingly the Shifters of Assjacket barely even looked up from their meals. Weird was our normal. I supposed a couple of bolts of lightning might make them pause, but a little indoor rain during dinner was par for the course.

"I'm certain she was just curious," Fabio said, clearly unsure if he was correct. "She's not exactly evil if that's what you're worried about."

"Define evil," Roy said, squinting at Fabio.

"How about this..." Fabio reworded his description at Roy's urging. "She's not mean. Wait that's not right. She's not insane."

"Not right either," Roy said.

"Okay, she's not vicious."

"Again, define vicious," Roy insisted.

"Fine," Fabio huffed. "She's right out of her debatably insane mind. She's the most terrifying woman I've ever come across. She has eye shadow issues and rumor has it, she enjoys turning warlocks into chia pets."

"Not a rumor," Bermangoggleshitz cut in. "My school chum Dirk was a chia playful puppy for a century."

"You guys are for real?" I questioned, completely freaked out. Had this whack job been secretly visiting my babies?

"Ask Marge," Sassy said, pointing to the door.

Whipping my head around to the entrance, I spotted Marge coming through the door carrying an enormous basket of cookies. She always baked when she was stressed out. From the size of her basket of goodies, she was very stressed out.

The Shifters were on their feet immediately and swarmed Marge like she was a rock star. While Wanda was the best baker I'd ever had the honor of knowing—her cheesecakes brought tears to my eyes—Marge's cookies were the best in the farking Universe.

"I'll get her," Sassy announced as she got up from the table and powered through the crowd of cookie lovers.

"Will she know if her mother has been here?" I asked.

"No clue," Fabio said. "But I certainly hope there are a few cookies left when she gets to the table."

"ENDORA WAS *HERE*? IN ASSJACKET?" MARGE CHOKED OUT, scanning the diner in horror. "Are you certain?"

I was concerned before. Now I was headed toward basket case.

"I don't see how she could have come here undetected," I said, confused. "The town is warded and Mac can sense outside magic."

"Wrinkles," Marge whispered. "She's the one who taught me to make a wrinkle. They're virtually undetectable."

"Do you think Elhora is making the wrinkles that Baba Yaga is worried about?" Sassy asked, shoving cookies in her mouth.

My BFF was a stress eater. So was I. It was a damned good thing that witches had ridiculously fast metabolism. Knocking Sassy's hand out of the basket, I took my own pile of sugar to consume.

"What did you just call her?" Roy asked with a pained wince and another quick glance around the diner while trying not to laugh.

Clearly Endora wasn't a laughing matter.

"Oh, sorry," Sassy said with her mouth full. "I meant Fedora... I think. Or was it Oxymora? Angora? No wait. I've got it. Menorah."

"Try pain in the aura," Marge muttered, so disturbed by the thought of her mother being in the vicinity she was leaning on Bermangoggleshitz for comfort and support.

Covertly, I cocked my head to the side to get his attention. Lifting my arm, I put it around Mac so Roy would get the hint. I knew there was a chance he would lose his arm if he put it around Marge, but he had to start somewhere.

Looking scared shitless, Bermangoggleshitz awkwardly moved his arm to the back of the chair she was sitting on. I was pretty sure he wasn't touching her. Good enough for now. His arm was still attached to his body and Marge was too scattered to even realize what he'd done.

"She messes with auras?" Fabio asked, disturbed by the news. "That's forbidden."

Nodding, Marge grabbed a cookie for herself and then passed the basket around. "There's a reason Carol and I are like we are. She wasn't exactly warm and motherly."

"Understatement," Bermangoggleshitz muttered under his breath.

"Well, Goddess in a naked clogging contest," Sassy yelled. "You and Baba Yofreaky have more in common with Zelda and me than I'd thought."

Sassy's statement was actually kind of profound and I realized she was correct. My mother, for lack of a better word, wasn't real good at her job and Sassy's had gotten rid of her when she was a little girl. Clearly Baba Yaga and Marge had similar experiences to what we'd had. Holy Hell... was that part of the requirement of being in charge having crappy mothers?

"Yes," Marge said absently, taking the basket and putting it on her lap so she could eat her way back to rational thought. "Suffice it to say it was... bad."

"She played with your auras?" Mac asked, appalled.

Playing with auras was against every magical rule in existence. It was punishable by death. How could Endora have gotten away with something so heinous? Why hadn't the Goddess intervened?

Marge's eyes were on me and I could swear she was reading my thoughts.

"The Goddess didn't know," Marge said, still looking directly at me. "And even if she had, some things have to play out so we can become who we're supposed to be."

Shit, she *could* read my mind. That was tremendously sucky. I'd always had a feeling Baba Yaga could do the same thing.

"That's rude," I told Marge.

She shrugged and pursed her lips. "I don't do it often, but you think loud."

"Umm... I'm lost," Sassy said narrowing her eyes at Marge and me. "While I understand that's not a surprise to anyone including me, I feel like I'm being left out here."

"Marge read my mind."

"Oh shit," Sassy choked out, putting her hands on her head to trap her thoughts inside. "That's not good."

Marge sighed and let her head fall to her hands. "I hardly ever do it. It is rude, and quite honestly, it's alarming to know what others are thinking."

As everyone at the table digested this new icky development, Roy leaned forward and got right to the point.

"How much damage did she do to you and Carol?" he asked. "And could you feel her if she was here?"

"Define damage," Marge said quietly. "And as to whether I'd know if she was here, no. If she wanted me to know, then yes. Otherwise… no."

"Zelda," Wanda said, approaching our table with a funny look on her lovely face. "Sweetie, your cats are causing the customers to leave. I hate to interrupt, but could you do something about that?"

It was almost a relief to go back to my normal where my familiars were having at their balls and making people ill. The habit was disgusting, but right now it made me grin.

"Yep. I'm sorry Wanda. They have no manners," I said, getting up and striding over to where Fat Bastard, Boba Fett and Jango Fett were participating in their after dinner ball sack cleanse.

"Doll face," Fat Bastard said with a wide kitty grin. "Wazz goin' down?"

"Apparently you are. Get your heads out of your crotches. The customers are puking," I snapped.

"Don't see no customers," Jango said, taking a quick lick break.

He was correct. They had successfully cleared out the diner. Even Wanda and DeeDee had high tailed it out. It was just my little dinner posse, Jeeves, and my rotund ball lickers.

"Youse furry shits did good work," Fat Bastard told his comrades as he gave his testes one last swipe and then waddled his bulbous behind over to the table.

"That was on purpose?" I demanded. What the hell was wrong with them?

"Sure was, Sugar Socks," Boba Fett grunted as he heaved his fat carcass over to the table as well. "Youse nimrods is talkin' classified shit in public. Wezze was just doin' our duty keeping your crazy ass safe."

"And you decided slurping on your privates was the logical way to go?" I asked, shaking my head and biting back my grin.

"Worked, didn't it?" Fat Bastard shot back, settling his big butt next to the basket of cookies and going to work on depleting the supply.

He was correct. My familiars were every kind of gross, but they were mine and I was keeping them. Actually, I was stuck with them. The numerous times I'd tried to scare them off or lose them in some random remote area, they always found their way back to me. Secretly, I loved them—not their foul and unappetizing habits —but them.

"You know Endora?" Bermangoggleshitz asked.

Fat Bastard eyed the warlock for a long moment and then smiled. "Youse is getting better lookin', dude. Youse better watch out. Soon youse gonna have de ladies wantin' a piece of dat."

Marge stiffened in outrage but tamped it back immediately. I noticed. Roy noticed and Fat Bastard definitely noticed. However, I would hazard a guess that's what my idiot cat was aiming for. The feline worked in obnoxious, gross and slightly mysterious ways...

"And yep. I knows dat batshit crazy wench," Fat Bastard went on as he began to lick the crumbs from the bottom of the now empty basket.

"Has she been here?" Mac asked, handing my cat a partially eaten cookie so he would stop licking the wicker. The sound was awful.

"Now dat I can't tell ya. Dat atomic turd raidin' hooker is a slippery one. Youse is gonna need Baba Yofineass to figure dat one out."

"Where is Carol?" I asked my dad. I assumed he would know since she *was* his gal pal.

"Not sure," he admitted. He ran his hands through his red hair that matched mine in distress. His expression was so serious I felt my stomach clench. "She normally checks in, but I haven't heard from her in a few days. She thought she was getting close to finding what she was after."

"Did she know what she was after?" Sassy took the question out of my mouth.

"Youse mean does Baba Yosexy know Endora is connected to dem wrinkles?"

Sassy looked confused. "Zelda, is that what I meant?" she questioned me.

"Yep. It's exactly what you meant and it was an excellent question," I replied to her delight.

"I don't know if she's aware that Endora is possibly connected," Fabio said. "I would think she would have told me."

"Unless she's protecting you," Marge said quietly. "Endora would hate for Carol to be happy. She'd destroy anything that made her smile."

"Is Baba Yaga working alone?" Jeeves asked, coming out of the kitchen and joining the conversation.

Jeeves had supersonic hearing like the rest of the Shifters. They could hear pin drop in the next town over. It was actually a good thing my cats had cleared the diner. Their style left a lot to be desired, but their instincts were impeccable.

Fabio nodded and then stood so fast, he knocked his chair to the ground. "I have to find her. Now."

"Hang on dere, Crapass," Boba Fett said with a chuckle. "Not so fast."

"How did you know his new name is Crapass?" I asked my smirking cat.

"De cats know all, Sugar Boobs," he said cryptically.

Of course now I wondered if they'd suggested to Henry and Audrey that my dad's name should be Crapass, but decided to let it go. If that turned out to be the case, turnabout was fair play. I was quite certain Fabio could come up with some lovely distasteful names for my kids to call the cats.

"Whatever," I said, trying not to laugh. "You will not refer to my boobs ever again if you want to keep your balls. Am I clear?"

"Youse is no fun," Fat Bastard said, making his rounds on the table looking for crumbs now that he'd pilfered everyone's cookie pile. "Weeze will go with Crapass to find Baba Yohotpants."

"Bad idea," Fabio said, moving to leave. "You'll slow me down."

In a blink of an eye, my obese furry nightmares were by the front door waiting for Fabio. For big fat felines, they could move fast when they wanted to. Usually food was involved, but a crisis merited speed as well.

"Fine," Fabio said, giving in. "Do you have any leads?"

"Does the Goddess have webbed toes?" Fat Bastard asked.

"Does she wear mom jeans?" Boba Fett added.

"Does she get jiggy with Julio Iglesias?" Jango Fett rounded out the absurd questions.

Fabio simply stared at them—speechless.

"Listen you shitbrains," I snapped, marching over to them, but secretly dying to know if any of that stuff about the Goddess was true. "I'm about to cram a hat of ass on each of your idiot heads. You either have a lead on Baba Yaga's whereabouts or not."

"Weeze can find her," Fat Bastard assured me, laughing. "But I wanna see dis hat of ass youse is talkin' about. Jango would look sharp in dat."

Jango, not realizing he'd just been insulted and set up by his buddy, nodded in agreement.

"You find Baba Yaga and bring her back and you all can have hats of ass. I promise."

"Weeze will hold you to dat, Dollface," Boba said.

And with that, the four of them disappeared in a blast of bright orange magic.

"So what's the plan?" Sassy asked.

We were all silent as we tried to figure it out. As usual, my brilliant mate was the very sexy brains of the operation.

"We will all stay at our place. We can take turns guarding the babies. We have plenty of room," Mac said.

"Should we alert the town?" Jeeves inquired.

"No, not yet," Mac said with a curt shake of his head. "I don't want anyone getting hurt. We need witch magic to defeat witch magic. With Zelda, Sassy, Marge and Bermangoggleshitz in the house, Endora will receive an ugly surprise if she tries to pay a visit."

"I like it," Roy said.

"Me too," Marge said, realizing Roy's arm was on the back of her chair.

Ignoring it, she stood and hid her blush by busying herself with the empty cookie basket.

"You little dudes ready to go home and have a slumber party?" I asked my babies as I picked up Henry and Mac scooped up Audrey.

"Buzzsit!" they shouted and then broke into a fit of giggles.

"I'm gonna take that as a yes," Mac said with a grin.

"Should we fly home on the brooms?" Sassy asked.

"NO," everyone yelled in unison.

"Just a suggestion," she muttered as Jeeves took her hand and kissed it sweetly.

"It was a good suggestion, my love. But I think the cars will be faster and we'll all arrive in one piece," he said with a smile.

"And our nuts won't be in our esophagus," Bermangoggleshitz added under his breath.

"All right, let's go," I said, biting back my smile. I assumed that Roy's broom landing must have been as shitty as my own.

We had a plan. We had the magic. And more than likely none of us would get any sleep.

Of course my magic was still wonky to the extreme, but I'd use it without a second thought if I had to. I just hoped we'd all survive it…

"Dude," Sassy whispered as we walked out of the diner. "Do you think the Goddess really wears mom jeans?"

"I don't know, but if she does, we have something really good on her," I whispered back, looking up at the sky to make sure there wasn't a bolt of lightning headed toward our asses.

Thankfully, we were in the clear. The unsavory adventure had begun. I didn't want to start it with an extra hole in my ass.

CHAPTER THIRTEEN

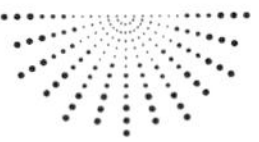

"Okay my little loves, it's time to go to sleep," I said, tucking my precious babies into their cribs.

Their room was everything I'd wanted as a child and didn't have. The walls were a bright, happy yellow and the squishy carpet was a grassy green. The ceiling was sky blue with puffy white clouds floating through it and a smiling sun peeked out from the far corner.

At night when the lights were out, tiny, bright glow-in-the-dark stars twinkled above their cribs. Turned out my buddy Simon the skunk had many hidden talents and was a wonderful artist along with being a kickass singer. He'd painted a mural of all the Shifter animals of Assjacket on the walls and it made the room even more magical.

Board books and stuffed animals finished off the living fairy tale and all the furniture was a beautiful natural wood. But the very best things in the room were my babies. Mac's and my wonderful, perfect, little foul-mouthed babies.

"Goddess, they smell so good," Mac said as he kissed Henry and gave him his favorite stuffed dinosaur.

Audrey slept with a one-eyed bear that had been Mac's as a

child. She dragged the sad looking stuffed animal everywhere with her. I knew it tickled Mac to no end that his daughter had taken possession of something he'd adored as a little boy.

"Mamma," Audrey whispered as I stroked her soft cheek with my fingers.

I froze. My eyes filled with tears. It wasn't her first word… bullshit was and Crapass was her second. But *mamma* was her third. And the third time is a charm.

"Did you hear that?" I whispered through my tears.

"I did," Mac said, kissing the top of my head and pulling me close.

"Mamma," Henry grunted, not be outdone by his sister. "Dadda. Crapass. Buwshit."

Mac's threw his head back and laughed. "I think you might rate a bit higher than me."

"Dada, dada, dada, dada," Audrey sang and clapped her hands.

"I love them so much it might be unhealthy," I said, giggling.

"Then I'm in the same boat, my beautiful witch," he said, patting the children's kittens, Lucky and Charm, on their furry little heads.

They took their jobs as Henry and Audrey's familiars very seriously and followed them everywhere. The kittens were just babies themselves, but they knew who they were there to protect.

"I don't know what I did to deserve them—or you," I whispered, watching Henry try to put his feet in his mouth and Audrey get comfortable on her tummy with her cute little bottom high in the air.

"I love you, Zelda," Mac said, lifting my chin so our eyes met. "I love you and I choose you. I will choose you over and over and over again. I choose you without hesitation, without uncertainty and in a heartbeat. I will always love you and choose you."

"My world," I said as I brushed my fingertips over his smiling mouth. "You and the babies are my world."

His smile undid me and I wanted to jump his bones and show him I was a *really* good choice, but that would have to wait. Right now I would simply bask in the wonderful feeling of being loved and loving him back.

"I'm on first shift with Sassy and Jeeves," Mac said. "You go get some sleep and tell them to come in here."

"Will do," I said, kissing my sleepy babies once more and laying a hot one on Mac. "Don't know how much sleep I'll get, but I'll try."

"Go," he whispered and copped a feel of my ass as I left the room.

Goddess, he was every kind of perfect—for me. I would choose him over and over until the end of time.

Eavesdropping wasn't really my thing, but Marge and Roy weren't exactly being quiet.

I'd tried to sleep, but nightmare inducing thoughts of Endora and chia pets kept crowding my brain. Not to mention I was still worried about Roger and his five badoinkadoinks. He hadn't been at the diner this evening, but thankfully I'd heard from several Shifters he was taking his new enhancement in stride. Simon had even shared that he'd heard Roger was seriously thinking of contacting the Guinness Book of World Records.

I was going to have to put a stop to that heinous idea. Besides, once I got a handle on my dark magic he was going to be right back to one teeny weenie.

So instead of sleeping like I was supposed to, I found myself hiding behind an ancient grandfather clock, spying on my guests in my own home. Not real good form, but I wasn't known for good form.

"I thought incessantly about your boobs even when I wanted to kill you," Bermangoggleshitz admitted to a wildly annoyed Marge.

Goddess on a bender, if this was how he planned to win Marge back he needed my help in a big bad way.

"Mmmkay," Marge said with an eye roll and a wince. "Try again."

"Umm… Even though I would have smote you dead in a heartbeat and laughed while you perished, the thought of your ass always gave me a woody."

It took everything I had not to laugh or scream. I was surprised Marge hadn't permanently removed his tongue yet. He was batting a massive negative zero in the romance department.

"Wait," Bermangoggleshitz said, holding his hand up. "I can do better than that."

Goddess, I certainly hoped so…

Marge crossed her arms over her chest and waited. Bermangoggleshitz's brow wrinkled in thought and he appeared nervous… or ready to pass out… or possibly puke. Heaving in a big gulp of air, he tried again. Honestly, he probably should have stopped while he still had a chance to make it to the morning alive.

"Although I would have happily torn you to pieces with my bare hands, I would have bent you over the couch and done you first. Better?"

"While that's alarmingly flattering—but mostly repulsive and disgusting—I'm not the one who up and left without a word," she spat, staring daggers at him.

"I beg your pardon, Miss I Write the Meanest Breakup Note Ever," he snapped right back.

"I have no idea what kind of crap you're spouting, but you are clearly trying to rewrite history."

"I think not," Roy growled. "I still have it."

"Have what?" Marge snarled. *"A woody?"*

"I always have a woody when you're near me," he shouted, pointing to the crotch of his tented pants. "Look at me. This monster is really hard to hide in public. My balls are blue for your information and your ass is a work of fucking art."

"Your *balls* can fall off for all I care and my ass is none of your business," she hissed. "You used me once, shame on you. Twice? Shame on me."

"I *used you*?" Roy sputtered, truly puzzled and pissed off. "Now who's rewriting history?"

"You are!" they yelled in unison pointing and zapping each other with magic that bounced around the room, broke a lamp and split the coffee table in half.

Dang it. I loved that coffee table. Enough was enough. They were incredibly bad house guests. I might be a bad host for listening in on their puke inducing conversation, but I hadn't destroyed any property.

"Enough. You zap one more piece of my furniture and I will go medieval on your asses. Or I might have to practice my dark genitalia enhancing voodoo-doodoo on both of you. You feel me, Romeo and Juliet?" I snapped, stepping out from behind the massive clock.

"Did you hear his *lines*?" Marge demanded.

"Unfortunately, yes," I admitted with an eye roll aimed at Bermangoggleshitz. "Roy, they sucked. However, Marge shitty lines do not merit zapping the shit out of my furniture."

Marge nodded her head and gave me a weak smile. With a wave of her had, she repaired what they had damaged.

"I'm sorry," she apologized. "Roy and I should probably be separated."

"We've been separated for centuries," he griped. "I think it's time to either talk or just off each other and be done with it."

Eyeing both of them, I shrugged. "Roy, your evil is showing and your horns are glowing. It's a really bad look, so I'd suggest you tamp that shit back. There will be no offing at my house. It's rude and messy and I'll kick your ass to hell if you try it—magic or no magic. And you don't want to test me. Ask Roger the rabbit if you don't believe me. *However*, if you're gonna talk, there are going to be some ground rules. And I'm going to referee."

"Sounds fair," Roy said, glancing over at Marge to see if she was on the same page.

"Fine," Marge said, glaring at Roy.

"Okay," I said, pulling the plan out of my ass as I spoke. If I couldn't use magic to heal Roy and Marge, I would try logic—or a loose definition of the term. "If you destroy any more property, you have to eat it."

Both of them gave me odd looks. Whatever. I knew that was a weird one, but I was serious about my house staying intact. I'd already flooded it. I was so not in the mood for them to burn it down.

"Next, you're each going to say five or two... or at least one nice thing to each other and then you will go to bed. The three of us are on the next shift and I would prefer both of you to be awake and alive."

"I see your point." Roy nodded his agreement. "Should I start?"

"Yes," I said, completely confident that he would fuck it up.

He paced the room and wrung his hands. It was a little heartbreaking to see how hard he was trying. Even Marge looked a little sorry for him... a *little*.

"Okay. Every time I've dreamt of murdering you in your sleep..."

"I'm gonna stop you right there," I said, cutting Roy off quickly. "I really think you should leave out all references to dismemberment. It's not sexy and it makes you sound like a total jackhole."

"Seriously?" he asked, genuinely surprised.

"Very," I replied.

Roy swallowed and closed his eyes in thought for a brief moment. Inhaling through his nose and slowly blowing it out through his lips, he gathered his courage and let her rip. "I fell in love with you because of your laugh and the fact that you could drink a sailor under the table. However, I'd like to add that your boobs and ass also helped tremendously. And even though I've fanaticized about holding your head under water until you were a goner, I don't think I want to do that anymore."

He looked at me to gauge if that passed. I thought about it for a long moment and then nodded. At least he had said he *didn't* want to kill her anymore. Or I think he did. "Marge, your turn."

"Although the thought of shoving you off a cliff and watching as your body bounced from jagged rock to jagged rock until a large one impaled you and you bled out has been a fanciful notion of mine for a few centuries, I was impressed that the size of your hands didn't lie about the size of your package. And when you recited poetry to me it made my heart skip a beat. Oh, and the size of your package."

"You said the package part twice," I told her, getting a bit squeamish at the direction of the conversation. I wasn't even going to touch the jagged rock shit.

"Yes, well it bears being repeated. Trust me," she said with a giggle.

Bermangoggleshitz was bent over in pain. I assumed his blue balls were now purple.

"Roy," I said, praying to the Goddess he was out of compliments. "Do you have anything to add? And it's *totally* okay if you don't."

Placing his hand on his heart and staring straight at Marge, Roy spoke from his heart… or possibly from his groin. "Your cookies are ambrosia and the dimple in your perfect left ass cheek makes me drool. I would very much like to bite it. Not a bite that would kill—just to leave a nice scar next to the dimple. Also the fond memories of playing horny fake priest and horny fake nun has gotten me through some of my darkest hours."

"Really?" Marge asked, delighted.

"Yes."

"I have one," Marge said, unfortunately warming up the exercise. "While most of the time I dreamt about peeling the skin from your body and enjoying your screams, my favorite recollection of us is when you oiled yourself up and we played naked Twister and then I rode you like a..."

"Whoa! Okay, stop," I choked out holding up my hands in surrender. "This went wildly awry and I'm pretty sure I'm gonna be sick."

"I wasn't finished," Marge said with a frown.

"She was just getting to the good part," Bermangoggleshitz said.

"My job here is done," I said firmly. "You have both said what you would define as nice things to each other with only several mentions of murder. I'd say we've all made progress—or at least you have. I just feel grossed out and ill."

"Thank you," Marge said quietly. "You have many gifts, Zelda."

I was a little floored by her statement and actually wanted her to go on. It felt pretty good to be complimented by a witch as strong and powerful as Cookie Witch, but I was terrified if they kept talking it would degenerate into more naked stories that I'd need hundreds of years of therapy to remove.

"Yes," Roy added. "For being a massive pain in my ass, you are quite adept at healing—even without magic."

Again I was floored. Again I stayed silent.

Marge and Roy left the great room without another word. I'd given each of them their own rooms to sleep in, but I had a really bad feeling they would just make use of one.

I just hoped they both lived through the night.

CHAPTER FOURTEEN

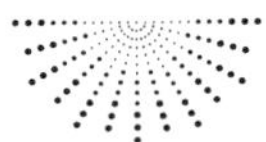

"Houston," Sassy gasped out, looking paler than I'd ever seen her. "We have a problem."

My laugh at her *Apollo 13* reference completely confused her and I realized she hadn't seen the movie. Sassy wasn't making a clever joke and we clearly had a problem. Thankfully I knew the problem had nothing to do with my babies' safety. They were in the kitchen with Mac and me, chowing down on chocolate chip pancakes. Henry was wearing more syrup than he'd ingested and Audrey had a big piece of pancake stuck to her chubby cheek. It was all kinds of awesome and adorable.

I'd taken the second guard shift with Roy and Marge. It had been wonderfully uneventful and my two cohorts had been unusually quiet and definitely still alive. I'd even gotten a few hours sleep and was ready to take on the new day—problems and all.

"What's the problem?" I asked.

"I don't know how to explain it," Sassy said looking pale and greenish now.

"Dude," I snapped, getting a little nervous. "Just use English."

"I think Profanican would be more appropriate," she whispered, nodding at Henry and Audrey.

"I'm on it," Mac said, clearly not wanting to hear Sassy's personal profane problems. He scooped up our sticky children from their highchairs and headed out of the kitchen. "I'm gonna give these pancake monsters a bath and then we can make plans for the day. Sound good?"

"Yep," I told him. "So?" I said to Sassy once we were alone.

"Sooo… I figured everyone was up and eating since I could hear all the laughter in the kitchen. Therefore, I felt it was safe to go borrow Marge's hot pick Stella McCartney sweater."

"You mean pilfer," I corrected her.

"Yes. Pilfer," she confirmed. "It looks much better on me anyway."

Nodding, I waited.

"This is hard for me. Do you have a plastic bag? I might hurl while I relive this."

Tossing her a garbage bag and a bottle of Windex just in case it might help, I backed away to the far side of the kitchen. If Sassy thought something was bad, it was probably horrific.

"They were in there," she choked out on a whisper.

"Who was in where?" I demanded.

"My Rad and Marge—naked—covered in pink frosting and umm…"

"Sweet Goddess on a crotch rocket," I gagged out. "Was there a Twister mat on the floor?"

"YES," she shouted and grabbed the back of the chair for purchase. "How did you know that?"

"Call it a really unlucky educated guess," I said, sliding down the wall and sitting on the floor. "Did they see you?"

"No," Sassy said. "Well, not at first. At least not until I screamed and took a picture with Jeeves's phone."

"Dude, you did not take a picture of *that*." I didn't know whether laugh or scream—or both. "Why in the ever lovin' hell would you want a record of Bermangoggleshitz and Cookie Witch getting jiggy?"

"I don't know," she admitted, dropping down on the chair and putting her head between her knees. "It's just so gross to see your Rad naked and covered in pink frosting while going at it with the woman who you wish was your real mother. It's scarring."

"Hence my question," I repeated. "Why take the picture?"

"In case I need to convince them to see my way on matters."

"You mean blackmail," I corrected her.

She looked pensive for a moment and then shrugged. "Semantics. That's a Japanese word."

My best friend had so many screws loose I was surprised her head didn't jingle when she walked. She was brave and clearly insane. She should also probably make an appointment with Roger for some therapy.

"This is certainly gonna be awkward," I said with a laugh. "How are you going to play it?"

Sassy jumped to her feet and paced the kitchen. "Here's what I think…"

Oh shit. Sassy and thinking always resulted in something alarming.

"I'll take the first baby guarding shift with Jeeves and Mac. You go and train with Marge and Rad. If I stay away from them for at least three hours and thirty-two minutes, I can pretend like nothing unusual and gag worthy happened this morning. Or I could train with you guys and unintentionally conjure up three hundred Twister mats and then hurl repeatedly. Of course I'd bring a puke bucket because I'm polite like that. I gotta say it's just wrong on every level to see your parental unit and potential gal pal play hide the salami—especially covered in pink frosting. Which, I would like to add, used to be my favorite icing. Now I'm stuck seeing my dad's joystick every time I think of pink frosting."

"And, now thanks to you, I will picture that as well," I grumbled.

"You're welcome."

"I was being sarcastic," I snapped as I stood up and began clearing the syrup-covered dishes.

"But you said thanks," Sassy pointed out with her brow raised and lips pursed.

"I was speaking Latin."

"Damn it," Sassy grumbled, snapping her fingers and producing a thick notebook out of thin air. "Another farking language I don't know."

She scribbled something down in her notebook, swearing the entire time.

"What is that?" I asked.

"It's my To-do list."

"It's a huge notebook," I pointed out.

"I have a lot of stuff to do. Are you going to be okay without me at training? I mean, will you be able to make eye contact knowing that Rad was licking pink frosting off of Cookie Witch's unmentionables?"

Goddess, I was so tempted to zap her mouth shut for a week or ten, but I couldn't risk it. Imagining what my farked up magic could do to a female was enough for me to swallow my need to mute Sassy. But it wasn't easy.

"Again, thanks to you, no."

"Was that Latin again?" she inquired with her pencil poised above her notebook.

Heaving out a huge sigh, I let my head fall back on my shoulders. "Yes, that was Latin. Now I'd suggest you disappear. I hear the Sugary Twister Duo heading toward the kitchen."

In a hot second, Sassy had disappeared in a flash of pink sparkles taking her To-do list with her. Closing my eyes, I tried to block out our entire conversation. It was going to be next to impossible not to give them shit—let alone make eye contact.

Whatever. Getting a grip on my dark magic was far more important than keeping my breakfast down.

CHAPTER FIFTEEN

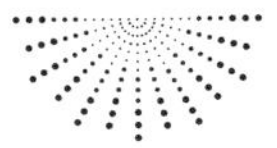

"Try again," Bermangoggleshitz commanded, clearly getting frustrated with me.

He paced the backyard and ran his hands through his hair. And if I wasn't mistaken—and I wasn't—his fingers got tangled in pink frosting. Gross. However, Roy's vexation with my lack of control didn't hold a candle to my own. I was ready to kick my own ass or give up.

"I don't get it," I shouted as I made yet another huge crater in my backyard. I was up to six now. "I didn't have this problem with my dark magic until a freakin' week ago. I was fine and then… not."

Marge stood off to the side of the yard. She'd put a good amount of distance between herself and me. She was a smart witch.

"Did anything out of the ordinary happen last week?" she questioned.

Marge was organized and precise. She was a baker for the love of the Goddess. She was a list person—one who probably did all the things on her lists. Not to mention, she was also the only maker of the green goop that helped keep the magical balance in our world.

"Dude," I huffed, exasperated. "Define *out of the ordinary*. We're witches. We live amongst people who turn into animals. My lumpy-assed cats talk. Not real sure I understand the question."

Marge laughed and crossed the yard. Taking my hands in hers, she gently squeezed them. "Darling child, everything you just said is *our* ordinary. I meant anything strange—unsettling—something that felt off."

"She has a point," Bermangoggleshitz chimed in with a curt nod of his head. "I am no longer getting the impression that you hate your dark side. Hence, I don't understand why you can't control it."

"Correct on the not hating it. No clue on why I can't restrain it," I said.

I didn't hate it at all. In fact, I was grateful for it now that I knew there might be a threat to my children. However, I still didn't have a handle on it and didn't know why.

"Baba Yocraycray said if I can't control my dark side it will control me," I said, searching Marge and Roy's faces for a clue as to how to be in charge of my dark mojo.

They said nothing—simply exchanged worried glances. It wasn't exactly reassuring. Was I stuck like this? Was I going to be a permanent liability to my town, my people… my children?

"I refuse to accept that I can't control this shit," I announced, marching farther away from the house. "I'm gonna try a spell."

"Do it," Roy said. "Just aim it north—and low. You have a lot of nice trees."

"Thanks for the vote of confidence, Buttmunch," I muttered.

"You're welcome,' he said with a chuckle. "You can do this… I think. Just concentrate. And go from the gut. And trust in your instincts. And zone in on the enchantment. And follow…"

"*And* shut your cakehole," I said with an eye roll. "I'm gonna fall asleep if you keep going, dude."

"Fine point. Well made," he replied as Marge gave him an elbow to the gut.

"Here goes nothing," I muttered as I raised my hands and prepared to… umm… I don't even know what I was preparing to do. Not good, but I had to start somewhere.

North and low.

I could at least do that.

Goddess on high, got a little problem here.
I'd be ever so grateful for your mom jeans wearin' ear.
My life is so full and my blessings are rich,
I need you to help me make the darkness my motherfucking bitch.
I swear on my honor, I'll owe you a biggie,
And in case you didn't know… Marge and Roy are getting jiggy.
Yes, I'm caving to gossip, and I know that is cheap,
But I'm getting desperate, dude, I'm in over my head and ass deep.
Roger has multiple peens and my yard is a mess,
So stay with me Goddess and I won't tell anyone that you do the nasty with Julio Iglesias.

With a sharp wave of my hand and clearly no help from the Goddess, a blast of black fire burst from my fingertips and I blew a hole in my backyard the size of an Olympic swimming pool. I flew about fifteen feet in the air and black sparkles covered every inch of my body making my awesome red hair look like fiery soot.

"Motherhumper," I shouted as I crawled to my knees and examined my newest crater.

"Was it the fact she said mom jeans or motherfucker?" Bermangoggleshitz asked as he sprinted over to make sure I was okay.

"Not sure," Marge said, frantically. "It may have been the veiled threat about Julio."

"And how does she know about *us*?" Roy asked.

"I'd hazard a guess that Sassy told her."

I lay on the ground and stared at the sky. Ignoring Marge and Roy was easy. I had way bigger problems. Why didn't the Goddess help me? Did I have to go through this for a reason? Was I not supposed to have my happily ever after? Was my past coming back to bite me in the ass and giving up my happiness was my penance—or rather, punishment?

My heart felt like it weighed a thousand tons, but my eyes were dry. Loving as much as I did now had taught me something very valuable. I would give my life for my children and Mac. And if leaving would keep them safe, then I would do that too. It would kill me more assuredly than real death, but...

"Something isn't right here," Bermangoggleshitz said as he examined me for injuries.

"No shit, Sherlock," I grumbled.

He wouldn't find any injuries. Outwardly I was a little banged up, but I was fine. Now inside my heart was a different story... that was where the damage was.

"It's as if an outside force is at play, but that's impossible," Marge said. "We need Carol. Has anyone heard from her?"

"Nope," Sassy said as she ran out to the backyard to see what the ruckus was.

She hadn't waited the three hours and thirty-two minutes that she'd needed to be able to ignore the horror show she'd seen this morning. I almost laughed as she very obviously and studiously avoided eye contact with her Rad and his Twister partner.

"You know," Sassy said, as she gathered me into her arms and helped me to my feet. "You blew a perfect hole to build a swimming pool in. Would have taken the Shifter construction crew a month to get it so deep and perfect. You feel me?"

Looking at the large perfectly shaped rectangle, I had to agree. I'd always wanted a pool and now I was halfway there.

"You're a glass half full kind of freak," I told her with a small smile.

"Is that a good thing?" she asked, narrowing her eyes at me.

"Yes, Sassy Louise Bermangoggleshitz Pants. It's a very good thing."

Sassy curtseyed and danced around me.

"I just don't know what I should do. Should stay or I should go?" I whispered.

"That's a great song," she replied.

"What?" I asked, totally frustrated. I was having a break down here and Sassy was… well, being Sassy.

"Sorry," she said with a grin. "I was speaking Clash-ish."

And I laughed. I laughed hard. Sassy had just made a really good one.

"You got me," I said.

"I did?" she crowed with delight.

"You did indeed. But I'm serious. I think I'm a danger to everyone."

"I call bullshitorama," Sassy said. "And that's Profanican in case you were wondering. You are staying right here where you and I belong. You're gonna get a handle on this dark crap and in the meantime you can offer out your services and put in shitastic pools for everyone in Assjacket. You could make a few bucks and a bunch of Shifters really happy."

"Hello?" a familiar voice called out from the side of the house.

My stomach lurched and felt a little queasy. I hadn't seen this particular individual since I'd multiplied his man tool. If he'd come to let me have it, I'd take it. I deserved nothing less.

"We're back here," I yelled as I stepped away from Sassy. If I was going to get reamed out, I was going to take it like a big girl witch—on my own.

"Zelda," Roger said, completely out of breath. "Love what you've done with your hair—very goth and sparkly."

"Umm… thank you," I mumbled, biting down on my lips so I wouldn't laugh.

Roger was wearing a skirt—a bright orange and lime freakin'

green plaid skirt with a ruffle. I knew that pants would be an issue with his enhancement, but a skirt?

"Roger, you're rockin' that skirt," Sassy complimented him on his heinous look.

"It's a kilt," he replied blushing under her praise. "The new package calls for roomier attire."

"You're sure that's a kilt?" Sassy asked, cocking her head to the side and taking a closer look.

"Yes," he confirmed proudly. "Fat Bastard procured it for me. Said it was all the rage in Oklahoma."

"Fat Bastard lies," I pointed out.

"Yes," Roger agreed readily. "But I don't care. I love this look and think I'm working it with style. I've ordered these beauties for all the men in town—you too, Roy. I'm confident in my masculinity and wearing a kilt proves that. Also, it doesn't squash my bits."

"So you're not mad at me?" I asked.

"Not at all," he assured me. "It is rather unusual, but I'm getting used to it. My aim in the lavatory is sketchy at best, but practice makes perfect."

My mouth dropped open, but nothing came out. I had nothing to add.

"So I'm here because something rather strange is happening in town and I was hoping you could shed some light on it," he said looking a bit worried.

"What's happening?" Bermangoggleshitz asked, staring in horror at Roger's skirt.

"Well, big craters are popping up all over the place. The last one happened about ten minutes ago. It's the size of an Olympic swimming pool. Now while it would be lovely to have an Assjacket Community Country Club. I think the middle of Main Street might not be the best location."

"Impossible," Roy said, staring at me.

"Preposterous," Marge added staring at me.

"Fuckin' A," Sassy said, giving me a thumbs up.

"Shit," I gasped out right before everything went black.

The last thing I remembered was hitting the ground with a thud.

The darkness was winning.

CHAPTER SIXTEEN

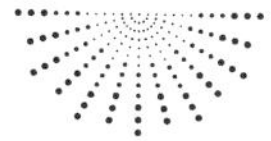

"I don't believe it," Mac growled. "I refuse to believe it. Not happening."

"Buwshit," Henry yelled and Audrey echoed him loudly.

"You see?" Mac said. "Your children agree.

Mac's eyes were wild and his wolf was very close to the surface. The truth will set you free but it may well piss off your little family unit.

The aftermath of the discovery of my multiplying crater issue was rough. Thankfully, I'd come to almost immediately, but I was now terrified of myself and what I could potentially do. Marge had taken over and made up some story that put Roger's mind at ease. He had scurried off back to town to assure everyone that the crater problem was under control and that the City Council should move ahead with County Club plans while my pool digging skills were in season.

Bermangoggleshitz was a freakin' mess. He stood in the middle of the largest crater muttering to himself. After her tall tale, Marge was pacing the yard, praying to the Goddess.

Sassy was the only calm one. My dingbat buddy was drawing

out the plans for a cabana to go next to the Olympic sized pool and had cleverly designed all the other craters to be a series of hot tubs named after the many languages she planned to learn in the next decade.

And me? I had made my decision. I didn't like it and clearly Mac, Henry and Audrey didn't like it either.

"Look," I said, pasting what I hoped passed for a smile on my face. "It's not necessarily forever. I'll just go to a remote place with no people and very few animals that don't mind craters and I'll learn how to control my dark magic."

"And where might that be?" Mac asked tersely.

"Probably Oklahoma," Sassy chimed in from the couch, still engrossed in her backyard design.

"Oklahoma?" Mac shouted, shaking his head in disbelief.

"The men wear plaid skirts with ruffles there," Sassy explained. "If Fat Bastard wasn't lying, I'm gonna guess that half the population has moved to another state. The skirts are awful. Trust me. I think it's a wise choice."

"Nobody asked you," Mac said, in a dangerously low voice as his fangs dropped.

"Sorry, you weren't specific when you posed the question. My bad," she whispered as Jeeves gently moved her out of Mac's sightline.

An angry werewolf King was not someone anyone wanted to mess with. Even Bermangoggleshitz looked uncomfortably impressed.

"Zelda, you are not leaving. I can't live without you. I don't want to live without you," Mac stated flatly.

My heart was shredding and I closed my eyes so I couldn't see that his was doing the same. "Mac, if I died. What would you do?"

"Follow you to the Next Adventure and yank your ass back where you belong."

My smile was sad. "Mac. What would you really do?"

He paused and stared hard at me and then he glanced over at

our babies. Sighing, he ran his hands through his hair and let his chin drop to his chest. "I would raise our children and make sure they knew how much their mother loved them. I would miss you everyday. Because if you died, my heart would die with you."

I wasn't strong enough to leave and I wasn't strong enough to stay. The only thing that made my feet move toward the door was the thought of harming or killing the people I loved—the people I couldn't live without.

"Roger will be stuck with his peens for a while," I muttered.

"He'll be fine," Marge assured me. "However, I'm in agreement with Mac. Leaving could be more dangerous than staying. I'm beginning to think someone wants you to leave."

I stopped pacing. Well, that was certainly a new puzzle piece.

"Roy, how many enemies do you have?" Mac asked, turning his laser focus to Bermangoggleshitz.

"Metaphorically or literally?" Roy questioned, completely serious.

"Literally," Mac growled.

"Ahhh, I'd have to guess that would be most of the individuals I've crossed paths within the last three to four hundred years or so," he replied tightly, looking embarrassed.

Mac turned away, walked to the wall and put his fist through it. The kids thought it was hilarious. The rest of us? Not so much.

"I'll leave at once," Roy said in a toneless voice. "However, if it was me someone was after, why would they be harming Zelda?"

I put my hand on Mac's chest to calm him. His heart raced and I knew he was ready to put his fists into Bermangoggleshitz. That course of action would have ended badly for both men and most likely our house. "He has a point," I said, standing in front of him so I was the only person in his sightline. "Plus, if it is an enemy of Roy's, we need him to help defend us with dark magic. Sassy is strong, I'm a loose cannon, but Roy is the real deal."

Closing his eyes and getting his fury in check with effort, Mac put his hands over mine. "You will stay."

I nodded. "I will stay."

"Fine. We need a plan of action for a threat that is invisible at the moment," Mac said with a grunt of frustration. "We can't rule out Endora and we can't rule out Roy's colorful past coming back to destroy him—and us."

Roy cleared his throat. "May I?"

"Be my guest," Mac said, warily.

"Sassy do you really speak and understand baby?" Roy inquired as Mac shook his head and looked for another spot on the wall to punch.

"I do," she said.

"No, I mean *really*," Bermangoggleshitz pressed.

Sassy paused and glanced down at her hands. "No," she whispered as her eyes filled with tears. "I'm trying so hard, but I'm not really that smart. You already know that, Rad. Why are you being so mean?"

"Dear Goddess," Bermangoggleshitz choked out, looking mortified. Crossing the room and dropping to his knees in front of Sassy, he took her trembling hands in his. "That's not what I meant, my child. I think you're brilliant and loving and beautiful. I thank the Goddess many times everyday for you and I'm doing my best to deserve you in my life. Apparently I'm doing a shitty job, but I'm trying. I only ask, because I want to know if Endora truly came to the children. It can help us rule her out if they know nothing."

"Why didn't you say that?" she asked, tilting her head and narrowing her eyes at him. "Were you speaking German?"

"Umm… " Bermangoggleshitz glanced around the room in terror, fearing hurting his daughter's feelings again. He was at a total loss of how to answer.

I wasn't. "Yes, it was German."

"Zelda?" Sassy questioned, looking at me expectantly.

Dropping my head, I stared at the floor. I wanted to scream or crawl out of my skin. Sassy could read minds like Marge—only different. Sassy actually went into minds and could see past memories. It had come in handy when we had needed to cross examine Baba Yaga's bobbleheaded warlock posse to find the traitor last year. However, there had been a chance that she might have blown up their brains.

She didn't, but if there was even the slightest possibility there was no way in hell she was crawling into Henry and Audrey's minds.

"What's going on?" Marge asked, concerned.

The huge gorgeous Great Room in my house now felt small and claustrophobic. Everything was going wildly wrong. I should have just written a dang note and left in the middle of the night. But that was the weenie way out. I was many things, but I was not a weenie.

"I read minds," Sassy said.

"Oh crap," Marge hissed and clapped her hands over her ears reminiscent of Sassy when she learned Marge read minds as well.

"Not like you," Sassy said. "I can crawl in and see the past. But I've only done it a few times. Not sure this is a good idea."

"What could go wrong?" Roy asked.

"Well… umm, I suppose if I screwed up the brain could potentially explode," she confessed with a wince.

Mac's growl of displeasure echoed my own. This was not the way to get to the bottom of what was happening. I wasn't even sure if knowing Endora had actually been here would help. The knowledge of the threat did not equal the potential damage.

"Practice on me," Roy said, stepping forward to the shock of all present. "I have vowed to defend Henry and Audrey with my life. If it's a rehearsal you need, I'm your man—or guinea pig —or Rad."

"You'd risk me blowing up your grey matter?" Sassy asked, surprised and humbled.

"I love you, Sassy. I believe in you. And if anyone is going to detonate my brain I want it to be you."

Sassy threw her arms around her Rad and sobbed into his massive chest. "I wish I'd had you my whole life. If you'd let me blow your head off your body by accident that means you would have never dumped me at an orphanage. And by the way, that was the nicest thing anyone has ever said to me. Well, there was the time Jeeves said he really enjoyed when I ..."

"TMI," I cut in before she ruined a bizarrely disquieting yet strangely touching moment with scandalous sex-capade info.

"My bad," she said, wiping her nose with her father's sleeve.

"I will volunteer as well," Marge said. "You may enter my mind."

"Seriously?" I shouted. "This is a bad farking idea and potentially messy. Marge, can't you just read Henry and Audrey's minds?"

She nodded. "I can, but I can't go back. I only hear what's in the moment. I wouldn't be able to tell if they'd seen Endora or what she might have said to them."

There was silence in the room as we all digested the distasteful plan of action.

"No," Mac said, breaking the silence. "Not happening."

I agreed with him. There had to be another way that didn't risk the lives of our children. My Goddess, I was ready to go to *Oklahoma* to keep them safe. There was no way I was letting Sassy crawl into their minds.

Wait, would I have really gone to Oklahoma? I had been thinking more about Alaska or the Yukon or Antarctica. However, I was definitely going to check into the population of Oklahoma. On the very outside chance that Fat Bastard hadn't been lying to Roger about the men wearing skirts, it might truly be an under populated state. And it was a lot closer to Assjacket, West Virginia than Alaska. Even though I'd promised to stay, it was smart to have options.

"I agree with Mac," Sassy said. "As confident as I feel with my magic, I won't risk the babies. It was a dumb idea."

"No, it wasn't dumb," I told her. "It's just too risky. They're babies—my babies."

"I still volunteer," Roy said. "And I think we should do it now. If there's an emergency and it has to be done, I'd feel better if Sassy got in a little brain crawling time. But Sassy, I will warn you now, what you see may not be pleasant."

"I'll only go toward the happier thoughts, Rad."

Marge stepped up next to Roy. "I volunteer too."

"Are you guys sure?" Sassy asked.

"Positive," Marge answered for both of them as if it were the most natural thing for her to do so.

Putting down her design slash To-do notebook, Sassy centered herself and slowly approached her father. Gone was the flighty idiot and in her place was a powerful, beautiful witch. Her blonde hair floated around her head and her skin glowed. Placing her hands on Bermangoggleshitz's temples, she leaned in and kissed his forehead.

"Relax, Rad," she whispered in a voice full of confidence and love. "Let me in."

The enchantment that floated around the room was golden in color and laced with hints of pink. It tickled my nose and calmed my soul. Roy smiled as Sassy wandered around his memories. She was as still as if she was in a trance and her brow was wrinkled in deep thought.

As quickly as she'd gone in, she came out.

"Are you okay, Rad?" she asked in a strange tone.

"I am," he said, watching her warily. "Are you?"

She nodded and lovingly stroked his cheek. "I am," she said quietly.

Marge stepped up and waited her turn. She had no fear on her face at all. She seemed quite delighted that the one who had been chosen to eventually replace her was as uniquely as powerful as she was herself.

Sassy repeated what she'd done with her father, including the kiss on the forehead. Marge smiled while Sassy poked around in her mind and sighed with contentment. The magic continued to float around the room weaving in and out and leaving a glittering pink dust in its wake. Henry and Audrey were happily swatting at it and giggling up a storm.

As Sassy finished and stepped back, she eyed her father and Marge. "You two really need to talk. I mean *really*."

I was dying to know what Sassy had seen, but also knew it wasn't my business. However, she wasn't done.

"Misunderstandings can ruin lives. I mean, when I met Zelda in the pokey I thought she was a materialistic butthole jackoff to the max. I was wrong. She is definitely materialistic, but she's not a butthole jackoff—at all. Well, she can be a slight butthole when I borrow or *pilfer* her shit. Pilfer is a Canadian word—not shit. Shit is American. But that's not important," she informed her confused audience. "Here's what is… if I hadn't bothered to stalk her butt to Assjacket, I wouldn't have known that. My life would have been sad and lonely and I would have eventually moved on the Next Adventure thinking Zelda was a gaping hat of ass. I wouldn't have met Jeeves and I wouldn't have four grown chipmunk sons. Who, by the way, are like freakin' a hundred years older than me. I told them to all just say they were twelve and call it a day—they're short—it works. I don't need to be aged needlessly by kids old enough to be my fucking grandfathers. You feel me?"

"Umm, Sassy," I said. "Is there a point to this?"

"Yes… I think so. Maybe. Let me talk a little more. I'm sure I'll find it."

"You go girl," I replied with a smile. She was an insane motherhumper, but she was my insane motherhumper.

"So since we could all bite it tomorrow, I'd like to suggest you two have a heart to heart and leave the pink frosting and Twister out of it. You both have the story wrong. Just sayin'."

"If I may," I said to Sassy.

"Absolutely," she said, handing it over to me.

"I'd like to propose leaving all desires of bloody dismemberment out as well. Peeling skin off and tearing the limbs off people isn't conducive to solving centuries old issues."

"Excellent point." Sassy congratulated me. "And another thing. Your mother is a fuc-arking chunky bulge spasm. If she's been here, it's a very bad thing," she added to Marge.

"Has anyone reached Baba Yaga and Fabio?" Marge asked. "We need my sister."

"No," Jeeves said. "I've sent out a crew Shifter albatross and Shifter moles to track them."

"Seriously? *Moles and albatross*?" Bermangoggleshitz asked with sarcasm dripping off the words.

Sassy rolled her eyes and smacked her Rad on the head with her notebook. "Don't you doubt my Jeeves. He can go at least eight times every night."

"While that's wildly unnecessary information, I find his methods in tracking embarrassingly laughable," Roy said, standing his ground.

"Really?" Sassy asked, narrowing her eyes at her father.

"Really," he shot back, trying not to smirk at what he considered absurd Shifter behavior.

Jeeves simply smiled.

"Shall I handle this, my love," he asked Sassy.

"Nope, I've got it, babe," she replied.

Oh shit. Unsure if Sassy was going to have a go at her dad for insulting her husband or if she was just going to talk, I moved the babies to a safer spot and stood in front of them, just in case.

Sassy took a deep breath and let it rip. "The Eastern American mole smells in stereo. Because the little fuckers are blind and have little use for hearing, the hairy, stinky rats use stereoscopic smell to determine their location and the location of their prey—in this case Baba Yaga and Fabio. And since that crazy motherhumpin' witch uses more hairspray than anyone should be legally allowed to do, this should work. As for the albatross, those flying shit buckets can smell fish from the air. Men in white coats with horn rimmed glasses—also known as scientists, which is a Jamaican word—have found that an albatross will alter its course toward prey located well out of visual range. Again Baba Yobighair's use of Aqua Net will help matters. The winged douchebags can monitor miles-wide swaths even when they fly in a single direction or are inebriated—which they usually are."

And that certainly shut Bermangoggleshitz up. Jeeves grinned proudly at his wife and Sassy gave her dad a *look*. She then turned to her kangaroo and laid one on him that should have definitely taken place behind closed doors. I was glad I was blocking the babies view.

"How do you know that?" I asked, blown away.

"Animal Planet. I love that shit."

"Fine," Marge said with a nod of approval to Jeeves and Sassy. "Hopefully they find them quickly. If it is Endora, she doesn't fight fair."

"Dooora," Audrey yelled.

"Yes, my baby," I said picking her up. "Marge is talking about Endora."

"Buzzshit," Henry squealed with a giggle, pointing at the ceiling. "Dooora."

We all glanced up at the same time.

We all froze horror at the same time.

I was glad we hadn't risked Sassy crawling into the babies' minds because now we had our answer. She was perched on the banister watching the chaos below with great interest. I waited for a brief moment to see if she would say *Durwood*, but that was fiction. This was real—very real and very bad.

"I've come for my babies," she purred, examining her blood red nails with detached interest.

Her likeness to the character on *Bewitched* was uncanny… Wait, it should be uncanny. She was the character from *Bewitched*. Right down to the royal blue eye shadow and piles of red curls atop her head. However, I could see the black roots and heaved a quick sigh of relief. There was no way someone like Endora was a healer witch.

Her silk robe was a blinding bluish green and spilled over the banister like ripples of diseased water. Her expression was sour and her bright blue eyes were cold and mean. She zoned in on my babies and the sides of her lips curled into what I could only guess was a smile. It was hideous.

She was clearly very powerful. A hazy glowing green enchantment vibrated around her and pulsed in rhythm as she breathed. I'd never seen anything quite like it, but I'd never seen a witch like her either. She was scary, but she was fucking with the wrong witch.

I could be very scary too.

My anger bubbled within my chest and my fingers spit black sparkles. I didn't care who the hell she was. She was wrong. Dead wrong.

Handing Audrey to Mac, I saw Bermangoggleshitz scoop Henry up and hold him close. They were safe for now and I was farking pissed.

"They're not your babies. They're mine," I hissed.

She threw her head back and laughed. It made my skin crawl.

"You're unfit and I challenge you for them. They are the next leaders of our mystical world and as I raised the two in power at the moment… I call dibs on these."

"Can she do that?" I demanded of Marge.

Nodding helplessly, she confirmed yet another bullshit rule I'd never heard.

"Any witch can challenge for young. It hasn't happened in centuries. It was popular and became law during the Salem Witch Trials when so many of us were burned at the stake. Many witch babies were left motherless and there were fights to the death for them."

"I'm not dead," I snapped.

"Yet," Endora corrected me. "You're not dead... yet. However, you've almost killed many in your precious little town. You are—as I said—unfit. You may as well be dead, insignificant little witch."

"Dude, give her ten boobs and eighteen vag-jay jays with your dark doodoo and then I'll call in the Hooch sisters to Brazilian the livin' daylights out of her muffins," Sassy yelled. "She's a farking crusty ass spasm. Don't take that crap."

I loved Sassy like a sister. She was disgusting and every kind of fabulous. Endora looked alarmed and completely confused.

"Is she right in the head?" Endora demanded, narrowing her eyes dangerously and glaring at Sassy.

"Not even a little bit," I said with an evil little smile. "And she's my second."

"Your second?" Endora snapped. "What on earth are you speaking of?"

"As the Baba Yaga in training, *I* make the fucking rules, you old bag. And since Carol isn't here at the moment, I'm in charge. You feel me?"

"Can she do that?" Endora inquired, staring daggers at her daughter.

Marge stood tall. Her hands were shaking and she quickly hid them behind her back. "She can."

Holy Goddess in a bad B horror movie, I had totally made that shit up. I didn't know if Marge was lying or if I was correct, but I didn't care. If I was going into a fight for my life and the lives of my children, I wanted Sassy right next to me. She was insane enough to make it work or at least confuse the crap out of Endora as I went in for the kill.

"So be it," the awful woman snarled. "Tomorrow. At the witching hour. Here. Enjoy your last day on earth."

"You do the same," I snapped as she disappeared in a massive blast of lime green smoke and glitter.

"Someone find Baba Yaga. Now," Mac roared as Jeeves, Marge and Bermangoggleshitz jumped to attention.

"Will you be okay without us here?" Marge asked worriedly.

"Will Endora be back tonight?" I asked.

"No," Marge said. "She'll wait until the Witching Hour tomorrow. She has more strength then—as do you."

"Sassy are you tired?" I asked, pacing the room and trying to think.

"Nope."

"Good. Mac and Jeeves, you stay with the babies. Marge and Roy, go find my dad and Baba Yaga. I'm going to call in Wanda, Simon and the rest of the gang for backup. Sassy, you're coming with me. You're gonna help me get a grip on my dark doodoo or else we'll end up with a pool the size of a small ocean in the backyard."

"Sounds good to me," she said, saluting me. "Just let me get some Windex. I think it might help."

Mac took me in his arms and held me tight. "You can do this," he whispered. "I believe in you. I trust you. I love you and I choose you."

"I love you more," I whispered back.

"Not possible," he said with a grin. "Go make that dark doodoo your bitch. You've got this."

"Everyone know what they're doing?" I asked as Sassy ran back into the room with three bottles of window cleaner and her notebook.

A chorus of yesses rang out and I nodded. I sure as hell wished I did...

"Bussshit!" Henry shouted and clapped his hands. "Mama."

"Mama," Audrey seconded. "Wuv Mamma."

My eyes watered and I kissed their sweet, smiling faces. "Mama loves you too."

And I was going to prove it.

CHAPTER SEVENTEEN

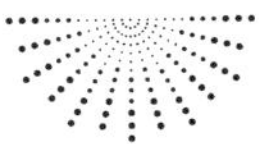

It was four in the morning and we were both exhausted. I'd gotten so pissed at myself, I'd almost taken a swig of Windex. I mean, if Sassy was so keen on the blue crap maybe it would help. Thankfully the smell of it made me rethink that stupid plan of action.

"Maybe the Assjacket Country Club should be in your backyard," Sassy suggested, trying to find something positive about the sad fact I'd blasted holes for six Olympic sized swimming pools.

"I have to learn to control this—there's no other choice. I mean maybe I could blast a hole in Endora, but my aim is so off I don't know what I'd hit," I said, feeling desperate.

"Maybe if you just give her twenty sets of knockers, the weight of them would make her keep falling flat on her face. It would give you an advantage."

I stared at her with my mouth open—no words would come out. She just grinned. Sassy was totally serious. It was the worst idea I'd ever heard. However, I tucked it into the *backup plan area* in my brain. If all else failed I would give Operation Booby a shot.

"Do you even know what a challenge entails?" I asked her.

Sassy was appalled by my question. "Holy shit! You have to wear a tail?"

"No, dude," I said with a half-assed eye roll. I was too tired to make it really good. "What exactly do I do during a challenge?"

Sassy paused and then shrugged. "We probably should have asked Marge that question before she took off. We might be a little fucked here."

"Ya think?" I snapped.

"Do you *have* to use magic? I mean your enchantment balance is totally off. Not sure if you can win a challenge—whatever the fark a challenge even is."

That gave me pause. Did I have to use magic? My balance *was* totally screwed. Even my light magic was wonked.

"I don't know," I admitted. "It is my house. Maybe I can make my own rules."

It was a long shot, but desperate times called for insane measures.

"How about a cuss off? You would totally win that," she suggested.

Caught between feeling total terror and complete helplessness, I laughed. My certifiable BFF could lighten even the most horrific moments. The thought of having a cuss off with Endora was absurd. However, I filed that sucker away as well.

We sat in silence and stared at the moon and the millions of glittering stars in the sky. The cool evening breeze smelled sweet and clean. It tickled my nose and brought a small sad smile to my lips. How in the Goddess's name could there be such beauty when my world was crashing around my ears?

"Are you opposed to kinda, sorta bending the rules?" Sassy asked.

I considered her question long and hard. I was totally opposed to cheating—or bending the rules. I hated cheaters, but… the lives of my children were at stake. I would die for them. Why wouldn't I *bend the rules* for them?

"Explain," I said.

"It involves me cooking," Sassy said with an evil little grin. "And it might not work."

"Go on," I told her. Sassy couldn't cook to save her life. I didn't want to begin to imagine what culinary disaster she was going to suggest. Poisoning Endora with a Sassy cake would be a really fucking long shot. It wasn't like we were going to sit down to tea before we blasted or cussed the shit out of each other.

"Go on," I told her again.

And Sassy went on.

And I smiled. I was fairly sure what she was proposing wasn't even cheating. It might be a little *bendy*, but...

It was a potentially shitty plan, but we were two witches who already had criminal records for relatively minor offenses... and everything to lose.

"Should we practice some of that chair ninja shit Marge was doing?" Sassy asked. "We don't need magic for that."

Being desperate, I would have said yes to almost any alternative at the moment. If I really could make the rules, maybe there could be a magicless round...

"Yep," I agreed. "Your brilliance is showing this evening."

Sassy's smile was wide as she conjured up two chairs and some rope. We spent the next three hours mastering *The Marge* as we named it. It wasn't as pretty as what Marge had done to Roy, but we were pretty damn scary with our chairs when we finished—not to mention severely bruised and sore. But I felt more confident. Bermangoggleshitz had said that a split second could be the difference between life and death.

I was ready... I hoped. If the split second presented itself, I was gonna take it.

~

OUR ENTIRE HOUSE WAS SURROUNDED BY SHIFTERS WEARING *KILTS*. IT was mind-boggling. Even the women were wearing them. The sea of ruffled lime green and orange plaid was so alarming it made me laugh with joy. My beautiful people had unknowingly created a heinous eyesore that might come in handy.

The babies were tucked safely inside the house. Mac's brother Jacob was guarding them, along with Wanda, Simon and DeeDee. I felt good about that. They weren't witches, but the sheer brute power they had between them was enormous. When shifted and in deer form, DeeDee's hind legs could kick someone into the next town. Simon's skunk could temporarily blind someone with his noxious aroma and Jacob's werewolf was as vicious as Mac's could be. Wanda was organized and clever. In her raccoon form, she could move like lightning and her fangs were like needles.

The Goddess had gifted Mac with an affinity for the earth and he had magically filled in most of the craters I'd blasted into our backyard. He'd left the biggest one and a few small ones intact after Sassy threw a huge shit fit and begged him. She didn't want to have to start her design plans over. Mac was a little iffy about having such a large pool and so many hot tubs, but gave in when he saw how much the kids and I wanted it. He was a keeper.

I just hoped I was alive tomorrow to keep him.

Sassy and Jeeves had spent the entire day in my kitchen. There had been three small fires and the top of the range had completely melted. Sassy had repaired all the damage with a wiggle of her nose and screamed like a freakin' banshee when she'd finally felt she'd gotten the recipe correct. It smelled awful, but I wasn't going to complain.

When we'd explained our plan, Mac and Jeeves agreed in a hot second. Jeeves also said that in no way were we cheating. Using our Goddess given gifts was what we were supposed to do to keep our people safe. And that was a very good thing. We had found my very dusty and underused Book of Spells that clearly stated any cheating in a challenge automatically disqualified the cheater.

However, the stupid book didn't exactly explain what a challenge was.

Fucking. Awesome.

I just prayed our plan worked.

It was eleven PM and there was still no sign of Baba Yaga, Fabio, Marge, Bermangoggleshitz or my cats. My stomach was in knots and all I could do was pace. With only sixty minutes until the Witching Hour, I was still a freakin' mess.

"If I lose… If she kills me, you will take the babies and go into hiding until Baba Yaga and Marge find you. They'll know what to do. Henry and Audrey can never go to Endora," I said.

Mac nodded tersely and paced alongside me. "Should we try this out before Endora arrives?"

I glanced over at Sassy who shrugged and grabbed a vial. She'd been studying with Marge and knew the secret recipe. Of course she'd needed Jeeves' expert culinary skills to actually cook it, but the Goddess worked mysteriously. Jeeves and Sassy were meant to be together in all sorts of ways.

"Do I drink it?" I asked, looking at the green goop.

"Nope, I sprinkle it on you," Sassy replied.

"Not sure we have enough and I don't know how long it will last," Jeeves said in a worried tone as he bounced up and down on the balls of his feet. "If we use it now and it wears off, Zelda is in trouble."

The green goop in question was, in a sense, our witchy nuclear energy. It was created by Marge with good intentions, but in the wrong hands could be used for horrible evil. As Sassy was to eventually take over Marge's job creating and spreading the goop to keep the magical balance in the world, she had been taking goop lessons for a few months. It was riskier than hell to use the goop on me in my present state, but again, we were backed up against a wall. My magical balance was fucked and we were hedging our bets that the goop could un-fuck it.

"Fine," Mac said with a curt and unhappy nod. "Tell me your plan."

"Okay," I said, unable to stand still. "First, I pull a spell out of my ass and blast a hole the size of a football field in the backyard. I figure that might scare Endora off. Doubtful, but it's worth a shot. If she wants to have a go at me after that, I tell her that we start with a cuss off. My house. My rules."

"I found a bullshit ordinance in the Book of Spells that said all challenges have to start with dialogue. Twelve times out of seven, challenges can be solved without violence. It doesn't specify if profanity is illegal, so we have that advantage," Sassy chimed in. "Zelda can cuss like a champion."

No one had the energy to point out that her odds were screwy so we didn't.

"Right," I said with a shake of my head and a weak smile. "So I don't think either of those things will work, but it will buy time."

"Buy time for what?" Wanda asked as she gave the babies each a slice of her delicious cheesecake.

"For me to live a little longer," I said.

She nodded nervously and cut herself an enormous piece.

"So, then if all else fails I'll conjure up a multitude of mammilla and..."

"I'm sorry what did you just say?" Mac asked, trying not to laugh.

None of this was a laughing matter, but I could understand his dilemma. It was kind of humorous.

"She gives Endora a shitload of boobies all over her body," Sassy explained. "The weight of the knockers, especially if they are at least triple D's should make the old bag's balance as farked up as Zelda's and then the odds are more even."

The room fell silent. I really couldn't blame them.

"Look," I snapped. "I realize the plan isn't great, but it's all I've got right now. I'm not giving up, so I'm working with what I have. You feel me? If any of you have a better idea, let's hear it now."

Simon, Jacob, Wanda, DeeDee, Jeeves and Mac stayed quiet. They were either still digesting the horrifying scheme or they had nothing to add to make it better.

"Holes Mamma," Henry shouted with cheesecake all over his face and in his hair.

"Buzzsit holes," Audrey squealed as she chucked a hunk of cheesecake at her brother. "Holes. Holes. Holes."

Letting my head fall to my chest, I had to agree. The plan was full of holes. A tingle of panic settled in my stomach and spread throughout my body like wildfire. Breathing was difficult and I quickly sat and put my head between my knees.

I was going to lose. And in losing, the most precious gift I'd ever been given was going to be taken from me. Not okay.

"We cut our losses and run," I announced to a stunned room. "I can't risk my children. I won't risk my children."

Everyone stared at me like I'd grown three heads. I wasn't one to ever back down from a challenge. I really liked winning and I was as competitive as hell, but this wasn't a game. My skills were fucked at the moment. I wasn't even sure I could take someone as powerful as Endora when I was at full power. Right now? It was a suicide mission with unacceptable consequences.

"We have the green goopy shit," Sassy reminded me. "I can restore your balance—hopefully. Besides if we run, she'll come after us and for all we know there's another asscrapping rule that will screw us even worse."

"Sassy is right," Mac said, squatting down next to me and cupping my chin in his hand. "If witch challenges are similar to Shifter challenges, you lose by default if you don't accept. Let Sassy restore your balance and you go give that witch a new bra size or four to remember."

"Or ten," Sassy added, checking her watch and dumping the green goop into her hands.

I held Mac's gaze and absorbed the love and strength he was sending my way. He loved our babies as much as I did. If he believed in me and trusted me with their lives, then I needed to believe in myself as well.

"I can do this," I said, standing up and owning the fact I was about to go out there and give Endora a gazillion gazongas. It wasn't normal protocol in a magical showdown as far as I knew, but challenging me for my children was every kind of bullshit and it wasn't going to happen. "Slap me with that goop," I told Sassy.

"Now you're talking," she shouted as she began to sprinkle the foul smelling formula all over me.

"Buwshit. Holes," Henry grunted, pointing at me.

"Mama, mama, mama, mama, mama, holes!" Audrey babbled.

"I know," I told them as I kissed their cheesecake-covered cheeks. "The plan has holes, but it's gonna work. I promise. It has to."

"No!" Henry shouted, grabbing my face with his sticky little hands. "Mama gaga holes."

It was the longest sentence he'd spoken and I had no clue what he meant. I knew the plan had holes, but it was what it was.

With a smile that belied the feelings rioting through my entire being, I kissed my babies again and turned to Sassy.

"You done?" I asked.

She nodded. "How do you feel?"

"Clear the room," I commanded.

They did. Everyone but Mac and Sassy hightailed it outside.

Rolling my neck and shoulders, I lifted my hands and pointed at the bottle of Windex across the room. Flicking my pinky finger, a straight stream of magic shot right at it and blew it up, spraying the kitchen with the cleaning liquid.

"I feel fucking good," I said with a wide grin. "What time is it?"

"Five minutes until Witching Hour," Sassy said.

"I've got this," I told them with far more confidence than I felt.

"Yes you do, baby," Mac said, hugging me tight and giving me a kiss that said more than his words could convey.

Sassy danced around like a child hopped up on a bag of

Halloween candy. She sprinkled the last of the goop over me for good measure and ran to the open door.

"Should I bring some Windex?" I asked, starting to believe I should really watch *My Big Fat Greek Wedding*.

Mac shrugged, laughed and grabbed an extra bottle. "Can't hurt."

"Absofuckinglutely," Sassy said. "We're gonna need it to clean up the mess after you show Endora who's the boss. And it's not Tony Danza!"

Even now, when my whole world was on the line, Sassy made me smile. Silently thanking the Goddess for all my blessings—including Sassy—I prayed for her to be with me.

I needed all the help I could get.

CHAPTER EIGHTEEN

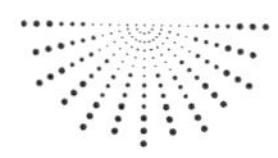

The first time she'd blasted me, I'd hit a tree so hard I was sure my brains had fallen out of my ear. Never one to let a little brain spillage stop me, I tackled the nasty piece of work and we'd tumbled into the enormous pool hole. At least I'd gotten two good shots in. The left side of her head was bald and she was sporting a few gnarly moles. But it wasn't looking good for me. Not at all.

I was fairly accurate in my blasts, but my power felt muted—like I was being drained. The green goop had worked great for about five minutes. Now? Not so much.

Mac, Sassy and Jeeves stood at the edge of the pool. Mac looked ready to lose his mind. I was well aware that his instinct was to protect me, but he also knew this fight was mine—and mine alone. I gave them a terse nod, to let them know I was okay. I hoped they believed it because I wasn't real positive about the outcome at the moment.

"Do you give up yet?" Endora bellowed as what was left of her hair blew wildly around her head. "Hand over the children and I will kill you quickly. Your choice."

"As if," I snarled and decided it was time to go low... very low.

Looking up at the star filled sky, I let her rip.

Goddess on high,
Hear me now.

"Oh pa-lease," Endora hissed with a cackle that would give me nightmares for eternity if I made it through the night—or even the next five minutes. "The Goddess doesn't have time for inconsequential, lowly witches like you. Do you really think she cares about one so sloppy and pathetic? One who can't control her magic and blasts holes in the middle of the pitiful town she is sworn to protect? One who deforms her own people? One who doesn't deserve the gifts she's been given?"

"Excuse me, you noxious over-eye shadowed assbasket," I snapped as my stomach churned. She'd hit home on that last dig. Sticks and stone might break my bones but I sure as hell wasn't going to let her words hurt me. Her magic was painful enough. "I was in the middle of a spell. It's beyond rude to interrupt a fucking spell."

"Wait a motherhumpin' momento—momento is Spanglish in case you were wondering," Sassy shouted from behind me. "How in the Goddess's mom jeans does Edog-gag know that shit?"

I froze and glared at Endora.

Endora froze briefly, then coolly examined her manicure.

But Sassy didn't freeze. She just kept on going.

"I watch *Law and Freakin' Order* and this is sounding very familiar, Bendora—very much like episode 4266435436. You know, the one where the wife of the millionaire is banging the plumber and her cat gets out and then her husband freaks out because he thought the plumber liked him—or something like that."

"There is no episode 4266435436," Endora shouted, completely confused. "And my name is Endora."

"That's what I said, Bigwhorea," Sassy shot back. "No way in the Goddess's toe jam should you know any of that intel unless… you were banging the plumber too. Wait. I got a little lost I think."

Oh. My. Goddess. Yes, Sassy was completely lost and I almost got lost in the millionaire- plumber-wife-lost cat debacle, but she'd actually hit pay dirt. How *did* Endora know all the things that had happened here?

Endora's eyes narrowed to slits of rage and she took aim at Sassy. Before I could think, I dove in front of my best friend and took the hit. It blazed through my veins and my scream hurt my own ears. Pulling everything I had left, I waved my arm and cast an enormous bubble of protection over my people. All my people, including Sassy. It was now just me and Endora—no backup.

Grunting with a furious anger I usually reserved for people who talked during movies and fuckers who ate the last piece of cheesecake, I called out the fastest spell I'd ever yanked from my ass. In my haste, I went with advice from my BFF. Again, desperate times called for insane measures—or rather risky, profane and wildly unheard of measures.

Oh Goddess please come,
I'm screwed due to scum.
From now on, true I'll be,
Turn the evil into a ginormous booby.

"So mote it fucking be!" I heard Sassy screech from the other side of the bubble.

In an explosion that enlarged the Olympic pool hole by about fifty feet, I watched in shock and horror as Endora turned into the largest mammary I'd ever seen. It was like a pornographic horror movie. I'd meant to give her a few extra sets, but it didn't quite turn out that way. It was one mammoth boob with short arms, short legs, a smattering of red hair on the top and a smooshed face where the nipple should be sporting a shit load of green eye shadow.

And it was mad. It was the angriest boob I'd ever seen.

Unsure if I'd won, I stood there and stared at the Endora knocker. Her oddly shaped eyes narrowed and she made a sound that was something between a muffled scream and a vicious growl. Her little hands waved in fury and she stumbled over her tiny feet.

Glancing back over my shoulder at Sassy, I shrugged and wondered what to do next.

"Zelda, watch out," Sassy screeched with eyes as round as saucers, pointing at the ginormous jug now rolling toward me like a fleshy bowling ball from the bowels of hell. "*Jump.*"

And I did. With only a second to spare, I used what little magic I had left and elevated. The boob hit the wall of the pool with such force it got embedded there. Endora screamed and sparked as she tried to un-wedge her newly rounded shape from the dirt.

My thought process was jumbled and I felt panicky. What was I supposed to do? The face part of the boob was smashed buried in the dirt. Was she going to suffocate if she couldn't dislodge herself? Was that a bad thing?

No, it was not a bad thing. It would solve a multitude of issues, but I felt sick watching the enormous bosom try to break free. Maybe if I poked her, I could free her and then roll the gazonga right out of Assjacket. That might buy a little more time for Baba Yaga and Marge to get back. I'd have to break the protection bubble I'd made, but the knocker was sparking like a Fourth of July fireworks show. There was a good chance if I rolled her hard enough she would burn right through it.

It was a tremendously shitty plan, but I was working at a disadvantage. I had very little magic left and a pissed off magical mammary. I dared anyone to come up with something better.

And then all hell broke loose.

The blast was massive and I was thrown about twenty feet. The protection bubble burst, shattering like sparkling glass around me. Amazingly I was unharmed. Waving my hands to clear the smoke,

I searched desperately for the booby. Coughing and choking on the massive amounts of glitter, I ran the perimeter of the pool with my hands outstretched.

No Endora knocker.

Where in the hell was the mammary?

"Yayayayayayayayay!" I heard Sassy scream. "Where in the Goddess's Spanx have you people been? Houston has a problem."

As the air cleared, I realized exactly who she was yelling at. Floating above the crater in my yard were two livid witches—a very pissed off Baba Yaga and a furious Marge. Their hair blew around their heads and their skin glowed more brilliantly than the stars in the sky.

Mac, Fabio, Bermangoggleshitz, Sassy, Jeeves and my cats stood at the edge of the gaping hole. Mac's fangs had dropped and he was holding himself back with Herculean effort. Fabio and Roy looked like magical bombs that were about to detonate and Jeeves was hopping around like he was going to explode. Fat Bastard, Jango Fett and Boba Fett looked like fat, squat, hairy demons they were so angry. Sassy was the only calm one. She gave me a thumbs up and grabbed her boobs to congratulate me on the monster knocker spell.

It wasn't their fight. It was mine. They knew it, I knew it, the boob knew it… and I hoped Baba Yaga and Marge knew it. I was pretty sure Endora had cheated, but I was unsure if two cheats would cancel each other out.

"I've got this," I said to my leader and her sister.

Baba Yaga gave me a curt nod and then eyed her mother with disgust.

Baba was dressed in a billowing gown of blood red silk trimmed in so many sequined balls she looked like an enraged Christmas ornament. Marge was in a gown of filmy silver with no extra adornment. However, she appeared to be angrier than her sister. She was seething and her magic vibrated around her, causing a waterfall of glitter. They were the most beautiful and scary sights I'd ever seen.

Baba Yaga snapped her fingers and the Endora knocker rose floated between them. She, too was fuming. The sheer amount of power of the three of them was enough to make me want to hide, but my children's lives were still at stake. It wasn't over yet.

"Well, well, well," Endora spat. "If it's not my worthless daughters. I've missed you terribly."

"What is going on here?" Baba Yaga demanded, staring daggers at her mother while biting back what could only be described as a shocked grin. "Time hasn't treated you well. That's the worst boob job I've ever seen, *Mother*."

"Restore me to my former beauty. NOW," Endora snarled.

"No can do, momma dearest," Marge said flatly, flying in a circle around her mother and examining her from all angles. "The one who cast the spell—the very same one you challenged—must remove it. And I'm not sure she likes you enough to do so. Trying to steal children isn't the best way to make friends."

"I will destroy all of you," Endora hissed, trying to clap her hands and cast a spell—which was impossible due to the length of her arms and the size of her girth.

"Yes, yes, yes," Baba Yaga said feigning a yawn. "I've heard that one for centuries and somehow I'm still here."

"Worthless," Endora snapped, eyeing her daughters with distaste. "You think you're so high and mighty because that ridiculous Goddess of yours chose you to rule, but that's because of me. Neither of you would have amounted to anything without me."

"Actually," Marge said through gritted teeth, floating around to go face to face—or rather her face to Endora's squashed boob-face. "We'll have to agree to disagree on that one. All the horrific beatings and degrading treatment simply made me despise you and leave as soon as possible. The Goddess was the one who gave me what you never did."

"Ditto," Baba Yaga concurred. "You've made a very grave mistake, *Endora*. In your current… umm… condition, you can't complete the challenge you issued."

Endora whirled in a circle like a fleshy disco ball and finally came to a stop when her eyes landed on me. "You will change me back and we shall finish. Do you understand me?"

"No, I don't speak Asshole," I replied with a shrug and a grin. I was buying time, hoping the green goop might just need a little rest before it kicked back in. If I returned Endora to herself, I'd have to finish the challenge. I had no clue if I could do it. My magic tank was totally out of gas. "Do you speak English?"

"I speak broken Asshole," Sassy chimed in, hopping into the hole and coming to my side with the big dusty Book of Spells in her hands. "Enborka actually meant that she's guilty of so much shit the list is too long to share and she really likes being a giant knocker. It would literally take years to confess all her wickedness. So she'd like Sassy Louise Bermangoggleshitz Pants to read her mind and then translate her crimes into English since most people don't speak Asshole as well as she does."

"You will die," Endora shrieked. "All of you will die and I will win. The babies will be mine."

Her words echoed and the trees seemed to grumble with displeasure. That was strange and unsettling. I'd never heard the trees talk and I could have sworn they whispered *at your bidding*.

"Did you hear that?" I whispered to Sassy.

"Hear what?" she whispered back.

Great. I was out of magic and now I was hallucinating about trees talking to me.

"You need your hands, Mother," Baba Yaga pointed out. "Your skills are nil without your hands."

"You're a horrid child. I wish you were never born," she hissed at Baba Yaga.

The flash of pain across Baba Yaga's beautiful face was unmistakable. She hid it immediately, but I understood it. My own mother hadn't loved me. She wasn't capable of it, but it had never stopped me from trying to win her love and affection.

"And what have we here?" Endora sneered as she took in the audience. She raised her brow, which was seriously grotesque since she was still a boob. "Roy Bermangoggleshitz… how *sweet*. I thought that was you last night. I'm surprised to see you after the unforgivable sins you committed against my daughter and our kind."

"I beg your pardon?" Bermangoggleshitz growled.

"What are you talking about?" Marge demanded as her mother's eyes grew wide with glee.

"Oh yes," Endora said with false sorrow dripping from her words. "She hates you. You ruined her life. She was banished for your crimes, you evil piece of shit."

"You're rewriting history, mother," Marge snapped. "You know nothing of what happened between Roy and me."

"He's scum and you're stupid, but you've got a vicious way with prose, *darling daughter*."

"Again, what are you talking about?" Marge pressed, quickly losing patience.

Bermangoggleshitz was fuming. His horns sprouted fire and one of his eyes blazed red. He looked every kind of terrifying—even Endora grew a little uncomfortable.

"Explain yourself, old woman," he roared at Endora.

Endora shrugged—again really freakish considering her shoulders weren't exactly where they should be. "It was hundreds of years ago. I really can't be expected to remember details, you filthy, sticky-fingered warlock."

Roy levitated and raised his hands high. Flames crackled off his horns and his dark magic shimmered and danced around him. He looked like a murderous, avenging, partially-beautiful angel with horns.

"No," I shouted. "This is not your fight."

With a furious curse, Roy floated back to the ground and

growled like an animal. Endora cackled and jiggled as she watched him stand down.

It was my fight, but I still didn't know how I was going to win. I had to prove the old hag had cheated somehow.

Sassy raised her hand and waited to be called on.

"Yes, Sassy?" Baba Yaga asked. "Does this actually pertain or is it about *Law and Order*?"

"I could save a lot of time here if I can get permission to go brain diving in a trash heap."

"Interesting thought," Baba said, staring at Sassy with a new respect.

Sassy cleared her throat and grinned, pleased with Baba Yaga's approval. "Furthermore—which is a Yiddish word—this pile of crap actually has some interesting junk in it," she went on, referring to the Book of Spells. "Says right here—possibly in Italian—if the challenge goes unfulfilled, the witch who is unable to fulfill her part for any reason must be sacrificed to the Goddess."

"You're shitting me," I said, hopeful for the first time this evening.

"I shit you not. And there is nothing specific in here about turning someone into a booby. So I'd take that to mean that Genworma is disqualified since she can't satisfy the conditions—a Swahili word."

"Was she dropped on her head?" Endora screeched. "She speaks rubbish. That is *not* in the Book of Spells. You're daft. And I am willing to fight. The red haired one cheated. She shall be sacrificed and the babies will be mine."

"Hang on there for a hot second, Boobzilla," Sassy said, beginning to enjoy herself. "I might not be the sharpest tool in the shed, but I'm definitely not the giant-sized knocker here. And thank you for making me aware that I speak Rubbish. I didn't even realize it was a language. I'm impressed my vernacular is growing without having to listen to that Rosetta Stone shit. Saves me more time for pool design. You feel me? However, I say we discuss your knowledge of Zelda's wonky power and her aptitude for multiplying genitalia—pretty sure that was Rubbish."

"Yep," I agreed, deciding not to ever tell Sassy that Rubbish wasn't a language. "Does seem a bit *odd* that you would know so much."

"Yes mother, would you like to explain yourself?" Marge inquired in a tone so cold I shivered.

"Turn. Me. Back," Endora said.

"Shortly," Baba Yaga replied much to my dismay. "Fabio. Roy. Bring out the babies."

What was she doing? Was she nuts? I wanted my children nowhere near Endora. Ever. Mac's vicious snarl echoed my displeasure with Baba Yaga's request.

Sassy grabbed my hand and held tight. Mac paced the side of the pool and never for a second let his eyes drop from Endora. I knew if she made one false move toward our children, he would break every rule and go for her. I would be right there with him.

Henry and Audrey were unusually quiet as they took in the scene. The entire kilt-clad population of Assjacket followed close behind. It was a vicious plaid sea of green and orange. The growls and gnashing fangs of my people made me feel very loved. My heart was in my throat as I waited to see what Baba Yaga would do.

I trusted her with my life and now I had to trust her with my children's lives. If she failed me, I would go after her as well. I loved her, but a mother's love for her children trumped all else. Maybe not *her* mother's love—or mine—or Sassy's—but *my* love for my children was something I would happily die for—or kill for.

"What do you see?" Baba Yaga asked my babies.

"Holes!" Henry shouted, pointing at me.

Well, I couldn't fault his observation skills. He was correct. The backyard was full of deep holes—pool and hot tub sized holes. My eyes shot to Baba Yaga and I glared hard. She raised one well-manicured brow at me and then turned her attention back to the babies.

"Buzzshit. Mamma gaga holes," Audrey confirmed the backyard was a mess.

"Where?" Marge asked.

My eye roll was involuntary and large. However, I didn't miss Endora's swift intake of breath and neither did her daughters.

"Bon Mamma, bussit," Henry announced. "Holes. Holes."

"Peeky holes," Audrey added.

"I've got it," Sassy yelled, startling me. "I speak Baby. They said Mamma's got holes in her bullshit and they're leaky."

Oh. My. Goddess. Sassy did indeed speak baby—kind of.

"I have holes," I shouted, shaking with fury. "*My aura*. You fucked with my aura. You've drained my magic. Sassy go get a chair. I'm gonna go all Marge on her ass. My house. My rules. You drained my magic. You will fight me without magic. I'll try to restore you, but just a heads up. Thanks to you, I don't have a whole lot of voodoo left, so you could possibly end up as a giant hairy wiener. You feel me?"

"Or five," Roger shouted from the crowd.

Endora didn't look quite as confident as she had a few moments ago. In fact, she looked horrified.

"Not to mention screwing with someone's aura is punishable by death," Baba Yaga added.

"Prove it," Endora snapped. "You can't prove it."

Marge glared at her mother and then turned to the babies. "Henry, Audrey, can you fix Mommy's holes?"

"Bushit," Henry squealed.

"Pucker," Audrey added, not to be outdone by her brother's profanity. "Love Mamma."

It was mortifying that the entire population of Assjacket knew that my kids had sewer mouths, but there wasn't time to worry about that right now. They loved me and I loved them. Potty words were just a bunch of letters mixed together that someone decided were profane. I mean, elbow or cheesecake could have been a filthy word if someone had deemed it so, right? I'd send them to Roger for therapy when they got to be two or so. It would be fine.

Before I could utter a word in opposition of getting my babies involved, I felt a warm blast of soft magic wash over me. My body began to tingle and little pins and needles came alive in my blood, waking up my power. It wasn't excruciating, but it wasn't comfortable either. My body jerked and spasmed and I could literally feel the holes of my aura begin to mend. That definitely hurt a little, but I kept my lips closed tight. I had no intention of letting my kids know they were causing me pain. They were going to need years of therapy to get past this evening. I had no intention of adding to it with unnecessary guilt.

As quickly as it started, it was over. Slowly rolling my neck and popping my knuckles, I aimed away from everyone and threw a fireball. It detonated with an eerie scream on the wind and singed the air with so much enchantment the horizon appeared blood red. With a flick of my hand, I extinguished it but not until its effect was felt by all. It was precise. It was deadly. It was gorgeous.

"And there's your proof, Endora," I said with a smile that didn't reach my eyes.

The Shifters of Assjacket hooted and hollered. It was a riotous sea of hideous plaid. I'd never heard or seen anything so beautiful.

A warm ball of white light glowed from within and warmed my soul. I felt the cooler fingers of my darkness wind around the light and settle in comfortably. A cool breeze began to blow and I laughed as I felt my power roll through my body with joy and strength.

"Just so you know," Marge said to her mother with a wide grin. "She's stronger than Carol and I put together."

"By a long shot," Baba added with pride.

Endora looked from daughter to daughter and then zeroed in on me. I waved and shot a little zap of hello. It landed right between her eyebrows and melted the bright green eye shadow right off her face.

"You want more?" I asked politely. "I've got plenty where that came from."

"I concede," Endora said, seething and shaking. "You win. Change me back and I will be gone."

"You will stand before the Goddess and wait for her judgment as far as your destruction of Zelda's aura goes and the denial of the challenge you made," Baba Yaga said to her mother.

"You will finally face the consequences of your actions," Marge said with satisfaction.

"Whatever," Endora snapped. "I'll stand before your worthless Goddess. There is nothing she can do to me. I don't worship her. You will reverse this spell and I shall be gone."

Marge gave me a tight-lipped smile and a quick nod. They knew her better than I did. I wasn't really happy about restoring Endora, but if she was going to have to stand before the Goddess, I really didn't want to explain how or why I'd turned her into a mammary.

With a wave of my hand, I restored Endora to her former self. It would be a stretch to say 'former beauty', but it was a vast improvement over the boob.

It couldn't be this easy. Could it?

Nothing was ever *this* easy.

In the split second between life and death a whole lot can happen. And it did.

CHAPTER NINETEEN

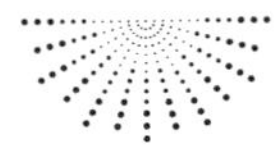

It was fast. It was ugly. It ended in death.

And not the death it should have ended in.

It seemed like a blur, but a hazy blur in rapid motion. I saw it unfold, but it was as if my brain was registering everything one second behind—and the person I'd least expected to save the day was registering one second ahead.

"Fine," Endora said calmly, checking herself to make sure she was no longer a mammary. "You win."

I heaved an internal sigh of relief. Outwardly though, I let my magic take over. Now that it was over, I grew furious. This horrid woman had come to my home—the place I loved—and hidden in time wrinkles. She'd drained my magic by piercing holes in my aura. She'd tried to steal my children.

Because of what she'd done, Assjacket was now full of craters, Roger had a pentagon of penii and my children had sewer mouths. Not to mention I'd come pretty close to seeing what the Next Adventure looked like.

Well, to be honest, the potty mouths of my children were my fault, but right now I was blaming everything on Endora.

A ball of fury simmered in my gut as I glared at her.

Shimmering gold fire laced with glittering black covered my arms and chest. I heard the gasps of my friends and even Endora appeared uneasy.

"If you *ever* try anything like this again, I will end you," I warned through clenched teeth as I held back the desire to blast her into oblivion. "You're lucky the Goddess will choose your punishment because mine would have been far worse than anything she could do to you."

Endora said nothing—just glared back at me with eyes full of raw hatred. Goddess, if this was how Baba Yaga and Marge had been raised, my heart was sick for them. Endora was spiteful and freakin' mean.

"At your bidding," something on the wind called out.

I glanced around to see if anyone else had heard it, but no one noticed. Maybe I wasn't completely healed. Had the trauma of my aura being damaged made me hear voices? I would swear it was the freakin' trees, but that was impossible.

"Why?" I asked Endora, ignoring my hallucinations. "Why did you do this?"

She shrugged and laughed. The sound was oily and deranged. It made me want to headbutt her or turn her back into a boob, but instead I simply waited. I deserved an answer and I would get it.

"I was bored and I wanted power. I deserve power and respect," she hissed coming unhinged, finally revealing something awful, but truthful for her. "You don't deserve those children. I am the one who created greatness before and I am the one to create it again. You," she sneered, staring at me with a dead expression, "even with your fancy bells and whistles are still nothing... and you know it."

"Dang, someone sure is a sore loser," Sassy muttered.

Endora snapped her focus to Sassy and began to raise her hand to do her harm. With a quick slice of my arm through the air, I zapped Endora so hard she shrieked in pain and swore. She swore pathetically. I could have *so* kicked her ass in a cuss off...

"If you ever so much as look at anyone here today again in your lifetime, I will make it so you won't gaze upon anything ever again. I love every single person here. Do you understand me, old woman?" I said in a tone so filled with rage she blanched.

Waving my hand, I pointed at all my people behind me—every single one.

"Wait," Bermangoggleshitz said, clearly unsure if he was included in my blanket statement. "You love me?"

"Figure of speech," I said to him while keeping my eyes glued to Endora. "You're here right now, therefore my responsibility—hence I have to love you for the sake of the argument. Capisce?"

"That's German," Sassy explained. "And it means she loves you but doesn't want to admit it because you're still a partial jackhole."

Roy laughed and nodded. It was actually charming even though half of him was still ugly. He'd grown on me the same way Sassy had—like a sweet smelling fungus that you could deal with most of the time and never completely get rid of.

"Sassy, you're correct, but I'd like to amend my statement. I do love you, Roy Bermangoggleshitz. When you make me do pushups, I hate you with the fire of a million suns, but other than that I love you. You're like the drunk uncle who doesn't help with dishes after dinner and tells off-color jokes, but we can't help but keep inviting you because every fourth joke is actually funny. Just don't spread my newfound feelings for you around. My reputation is already fucked. You feel me?"

"Umm, Houston?" Sassy said with her hand raised.

"Yes, Sassy?"

"Your rep is a goner. Everyone in town just heard you tell my dad you loved him. I'm gonna have to say you're no longer an uncaring materialistic witch."

"That's a really shitty thing to say," I pointed out.

"Wait," Sassy said, clearly rethinking her insulting description. "I take back the materialistic part. You are *totally* still materialistic."

"Thank you."

"You're welcome," she replied with a thumbs up. "And just for the record, I love my dad too—a lot."

"And I love my daughter and her insane friend," Roy announced, getting into the lovefest.

"And I love Roy Bermangoggleshitz as well," Marge called out in a loud voice. "I always have and I always will."

"Nows dis is gettin' good," Fat Bastard said. "Howsevers, Sugar Bottom, I think you shoulda left dat old crusty snot licker a boob. Just sayin'"

My cat was never one to hold his opinion back…

"You love me?" Roy asked Marge as all of the Shifters of Assjacket began to sigh, swoon and giggle.

"I do," she admitted with a blush. "But I will still make your life hell."

"I wouldn't have it any other way," Roy said, sounding several hundred years younger than he did only seconds ago.

His joy was unmistakable and I grinned. At least something good had happened tonight.

Endora gagged and rolled her eyes in disgust. "Give me a break. The filthy warlock stole your potion," she snapped at Marge. "And he used it to do horrible things. The world almost ended because you let that cretin into your life. And *you*," she snarled, turning her attention to Bermangoggleshitz. "I'd think after the letter she wrote you about all the other warlocks she was entertaining and how you meant nothing to her, you wouldn't be so quick to forgive. She told you she'd faked it every time and that your tiny equipment had never satisfied. She wasn't even sure you could call what you filthy people did fornication. It was that bad."

Well, that certainly shut everyone up—everyone except Roy and Marge. Roy swore and growled in fury as Marge gasped in confused shock.

"And that's exactly what I was talking about," Sassy said

with a grunt of disgust and a very pronounced middle finger aimed at Endora. "Misunderstandings suck ass. Hang on for a second."

While everyone was still digesting what Endora had revealed, Sassy walked right over to her, grabbed her by the hair and dove into her brain. Endora screamed and tried to get away, but Sassy was on a mission. And when Sassy was on a mission, no one could stop her. She wasn't careful. She wasn't gentle. Endora's screams were earsplitting, but I felt no compassion. I was beginning to put the story together and clearly Sassy already had. For someone lacking in the brains department, my BFF was kicking some major crainial ass this week.

With a grunt of revulsion, Sassy let go of Endora. The old evil witch fell to the ground and clutched her head in agony. She was lucky Sassy hadn't blown her grey matter up on purpose.

"Just as I suspected," Sassy said, going all *Law and Order* on us as she paced back and forth like she was making her closing statements in a court case. "The plaintiff is clearly insane. She is a rusty knob humper and a liar. Her victims are too many to name, but pertaining to this case being heard by the court, the victims are Cookie Witch and Roy Bermangoggleshitz."

Sassy then did the staccato *bomp bomp* sound effect from the TV show. I almost laughed but bit it back. She was on a roll and I wasn't about to stop her.

Sassy glanced down at the witch in the dirt and pulled her back up by her hair. "You will answer the questions. You will tell the truth or I will dive back in and scramble your brains so hard that you'll beg Zelda to kill your sorry ass. You feel me?"

Endora nodded her head and stared at the ground. Her magic vibrated around her, but I kept a close eye on that. Certainly she wasn't stupid enough to try anything with all of us here....

"Who wrote the breakup letter to Roy Bermangoggleshitz and signed it from Cookie Witch *aka* Marge?" Sassy demanded.

With her eyes still downward cast, Endora muttered inaudibly.

"I can't hear you, *Mother*," Marge said, stepping forward and beginning to spark like a small inferno.

"I did," Endora growled.

"And who tried to steal that green smelly shit and do evil with it, then blame it all on Roy Bermangoggleshitz?" Sassy continued.

"I did," Endora admitted.

"Why?" Sassy pressed, going for the jugular.

"Because it was fun," Endora hissed and the crowd booed.

"Sooooo… I present to you, my heinously dressed, kilt wearing jury, the following facts. Hundreds of years were wasted in misery because Enjackoffora messed with her daughter's happiness. If she wasn't happy, she was going to make damned well sure no one else was either. The facts clearly state she has been a shitty mother and I know shitty mothers. Trust me on that. However, I do owe that nasty assmower a small debt of gratitude. If Cookie Witch and Roy had always been together, my dad wouldn't have been a manwhore. Hence he wouldn't have popped my egg donor—whom, by the way, he can't remember—and I wouldn't be standing before you today presenting my findings and making the world a better place. I rest my case."

"You didn't write the letter?" Roy asked Marge.

She shook her head. "No. You didn't steal the goop?"

"No," he said, crossing swiftly to her. "I love you and I always will." He took Marge's trembling hand in his and his kissed it reverently. "Always."

"And they all lived happily ever after," Baba Yaga said, smiling at a blushing Marge and delighted Roy. "My princess sister finally got her prince. The power was rightly restored to the Baba Yaga *in training* and her miracle children are unharmed—slightly profane, but that's to be expected. The deductive skills of the one known as Sassy Louise Bermangoggleshitz Pants will forever be celebrated and remembered. Never again shall you think of yourself as daft—a French word meaning *not smart*, in case you were wondering," she told Sassy with an amused chuckle. "And the bad, evil, wicked witch was defeated. She will be punished by our beloved Goddess and all will be balanced and right with our world. So mote it be."

"Over my dead body," Endora shrieked as she pulled on her power and shot the largest bolt of magic I'd ever seen. "If I can't have those children, no one can."

The streak flew so fast and with such force, even at full magic I couldn't deflect it. My cats dove to take the hit but fell to the ground with thuds as the deadly enchantment whizzed past, headed right for the most precious things in my life. Mac's roar of agony hurt my ears as he too tried to take the hit. But the magic was so intense it blew him back and his effort was in vain.

Baba Yaga and Marge almost disappeared to the human eye they moved so quickly, but again in vain. Sassy's scream of terror echoed in my ears as everything went into slow motion and my heart shattered into a million pieces.

But someone was ahead of all us… including Endora.

With a roar that had to have been heard in the Next Adventure, Bermangoggleshitz appeared to leave his body and jettison his soul across the yard in front of my children. He flung every part of himself with an enchantment so powerful it left me breathless. The move was so abstract I couldn't tell what was happening. A riot of dark colors swirled and crackled. His aura was glittering black mixed with swirls of blood red and smoky burnt silver. It surrounded my children and pillowed them in a dark impenetrable magic that nothing could pierce.

His body, aura and soul had protected my children from the death magic Endora had shot, but he couldn't save himself. As the magic was deflected and exploded with a sickening explosion in the sky, Roy Bermangoggleshitz fell lifeless to the ground at the feet of my babies.

Sassy and Marge's screams floated eerily on the wind and Fabio dropped to the ground next to Roy. My father began to chant and pray to the Goddess in a desperate voice, begging for the power to heal him. I watched in horror as Bermangoggleshitz's soul rose out of his body and looked down at the scene below. He smiled with satisfaction when he saw Henry and Audrey were in Mac's arms alive—shaken but breathing, their eyes as big as saucers. Then his gaze traveled to Marge. His pain was so visceral, my breath caught in my throat. His ascension halted and his hand reached for her. She couldn't see it as she was prostrate over his fallen body and sobbing.

Then the wind spoke… again.

"At your bidding," it whispered.

Whipping around to figure out who was speaking, I saw Baba Yaga with her mother pinned to the ground beneath her. For the moment Baba Yaga was winning, but Endora was glowing a putrid, vicious green and looked like she could detonate any second. We'd already lost Bermangoggleshitz. I wasn't about to let his death have been in vain.

At my bidding… At my bidding…

At my bidding?

They wanted me to bid? Fine. I was gonna bid.

At this point what did I have to lose? A whole heck of a lot. I was going to call on all the help I could get even if it was imaginary.

"I bid you come to me," I shouted to the wind. "I bid you to bind the evil and hold it fast. I bid you to come to me. *NOW.*"

The rumble sounded like an earthquake. The wind picked up blowing my hair across my eyes, which was why I thought I was seeing things—like trees uprooting themselves from the forest and sprinting toward me.

Nope, not hallucinating. I had apparently called on the trees and they were heeding my call.

Flicking my hair away from my face, I raised my arms high and welcomed the insanity barreling my way. It felt right and I was going with it. I just really prayed I wasn't delirious.

I bid you to come.

I bid you to stay.
I bid you to help take the evil away.
With your branches, wrap tight the one who is wicked.
Stop this now, hold her fast so she may be restricted.
In the Goddess's name and white magic I bear,
In you I shall trust to end this affair.

The trees brought so much wind with them everyone was blown willy-nilly around the yard—but not me and not Endora. In something out of a movie even Tim Burton couldn't imagine, my trees bound Endora in a grip so firm I was certain her arms and legs would break loose from her body. The magic in the branches extracted her power and held it in a quivering ball nestled in the rustling leaves. Five huge trees trapped her and held her prisoner. Her screams were horrifying and I felt them all the way to my toes.

"At your bidding," the enormous oaks murmured.

I had no clue where the sound had actually come from, as they had no discernable faces or mouths, but I didn't care. Bowing deep, I paid homage to my new friends.

"With everything I have and everything I am, I thank you," I said.

"At your bidding," they sang softly and then gagged Endora's screaming with thousands of enchanted leaves.

Goddess, I was certainly glad they were on my side...

The only sounds to be heard now were the soft, heartbroken sobs of Marge and Sassy. My gut clenched and I approached the body of the man that had given his life for my children. Gone were the ugly parts and in their place was pure, unearthly beauty. In his sacrifice, Bermangoggleshitz had truly become good. Glancing up, I searched for his soul. I couldn't see it anymore. Had he gone on to the Next Adventure already?

"Bermashitshit sleep," Henry said, sliding down Mac and crawling over to where Roy lay.

"No, baby," I said, squatting down next to my son as he gently ran his chubby hands over Bermangoggleshitz's slack yet gorgeous face.

"Pizzess kizzy Shitshits," Audrey yelled, pointed at Roy. "Buzzshit Cookie."

"Bowbite," Henry added seriously. "Kizzy Shitshits. Okay. Pucker."

"Sassy," I said, feeling like what my kids had said was really fucking important—however, I had no clue what exactly they'd said. "Did you understand that?"

Sassy eyes were red and swollen with tears. She closed her eyes and reached for Jeeves. Nodding, she tried to speak, but no words came. Her screaming grief had rendered her mute. Son of a bitch. Of all the times for Sassy to be speechless...

"Marge, read her mind. Now," I commanded. "*Now.*"

I still felt the presence of Roy's soul, but it was weakening quickly and fading away.

Marge, put her hands on Sassy's cheeks and pressed her forehead against hers.

"The Shitshit isn't dead. He sleeps and waits for the princess to kiss the Shitshit. Like Snow White. Just kiss the Shitshit and all will be okay. Bullshit cookie. And the last part was either pucker or fucker—Sassy says that could go either way," Marge said and then jerked back in shock. "Do you think..."

"Don't think," I shouted. "It's completely overrated. Kissy Shitshits. NOW!"

And she did.

I held my breath and prayed to the Goddess for a miracle. We were really due one considering what we'd been through.

Way too slowly for my shattered sanity, Bermangoggleshitz's eyes opened. He looked disoriented and confused. His breathing was labored and he was clearly still in pain. His gaze darted around and finally landed on Marge and Sassy. A breathtaking smile pulled at his now beautiful lips and I was grinning so hard my face hurt.

"Oh my Goddess," Marge cried out and buried her face in his chest.

"Thought I was a goner there for a minute," Roy choked out. His voice was raw and sounded like he'd swallowed glass, but it was beautiful. "Is everyone okay?"

"Thanks to you, yes," I said, gently pulling Marge off of him. "I need to do a little work here. I promise I'll give him back to you in a sec."

"Pretty sure my genitals are fine," Roy whispered with a weak grin. "You can skip that part of the healing."

"Thank the Goddess for that small favor," I shot back with a laugh. "And just so you know, my kids have christened you Shitshit."

"I like it," Bermangoggleshitz said. "It's certainly better than Crapass."

"That's debatable," I told him as I touched his chest and closed my eyes.

I felt my power rise up within me. Relaxing, I let it flow from my body and into his. The pain that shot through me as I healed Bermangoggleshitz was like nothing I'd ever known, but I would have repeated it a thousand times without complaint. Not only did I love Roy Bermangoggleshitz, I would die for him. A little severe, intense, agonizing, fucking stabbing pain was a tiny price to pay for what he had done.

The split second between life and death was indeed short, but thankfully a second was still an increment of time. Time was a beautiful thing.

Bermangoggleshitz had given me time—time with my children. Time for my children to grow and become who they were supposed to be. And in turn, my children had given the gift of time right back to Shitshit. He now had the time to love and be loved.

As the sun rose on the battered inhabitants of Assjacket, we were all a bit worse for wear but had never been so happy. The sun burned the dark sky away and became a brilliant pink. The Goddess sent showers of silver and pink glitter. It rained down and covered us in blessings and love.

However, the goddess wasn't quite done. With a bolt of lightning violently opposite to the light magic that surrounded us, Endora was ripped from my trees and sucked into a tornado-like vortex.

The Goddess wasn't fucking around—at all.

"Good riddance to bad rubbish," Baba Yaga whispered as she clung to my father for support.

It was an accurate and succinct statement. I couldn't have said it better myself. However, it might have been stronger with some profanity thrown in.

"How did you call the trees?" Mac asked as he wrapped his strong arms around both of our babies and me.

"I don't know," I admitted as the crowd slowly dispersed.

Sassy, Jeeves and Marge helped Bermangoggleshitz to our house. He was walking unsteadily, but with the help of those who loved him, I knew he would be fine eventually.

"They're your minions," Baba Yaga said as she and Fabio approached. "I have bobble- headed warlocks. Apparently you have trees," she said with a shrug and a tired smile.

I was amazed how well her hideous dress had come through the shit storm. But then again, she was the Baba fucking Yaga.

"Umm… I don't understand," I said.

"Or possibly you don't want to… The time is coming sooner than I'd originally thought," she replied cryptically, giving me a wink.

I didn't like that wink and I didn't want to hear any more crap right now. If she thought I was going to take over her job any time soon just because I had some wooden buddies, she was smoking crack. I needed a freakin' vacation—not a new job. The Shifter Wanker was job enough for me.

"Nope. Not listening," I said, sticking my tongue out at her. "You aren't going anywhere any time soon, Carol."

"What a wonderful idea," she said, nudging Fabio. "Should we tell her?"

"Be my guest, my love," my father said, putting his arm around his fashion impaired gal pal.

"We're moving in together! I'm moving to Assjacket and I'll be your new neighbor," she sang with delight.

Holding back every rude comment that I wanted to say was difficult. Goddess, my maturity was truly appalling. But Carol and my dad looked so stupidly happy, I decided to just smile. Or I tried. I was pretty sure it looked like a constipated wince, but they seemed to buy it.

Life was going to change as I knew it. With Baba Yaga, Marge and Bermangoggleshitz as new Assjackians, it was going to be interesting—that's Fuckingscaryglish in case you were wondering.

EPILOGUE

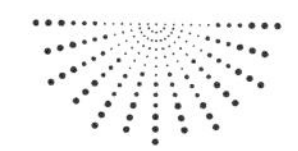

The Assjacket Country Club was everything Sassy promised it would be and more.

It was also in my backyard.

Today the official grand opening was happening in a big, splashy, joy-filled way. The Shifters couldn't give an asscrack that it was late October and a chill was in the air. A pool was a pool was a pool was a pool and they were going to swim in all of them.

It had taken a few weeks, a bunch of artistic debates—also known as Sassy shitfits, a little magic and a few mock episodes of *Law and Order* to pull it all together, but the results were worth it. Our backyard looked like a resort with more hot tubs than legally allowed.

"I'm going to the Canadian," Sassy shouted as she sprinted across the yard and hopped into the steamy water. Jeeves and their chipmunk sons were hot on her trail and they splashed up a storm in the Canadian. It was all kinds of weird and all kinds of perfect. Sassy had tried all fifteen hot tubs and decided the Canadian was the most mild and friendly. She was certifiable, but she was my BFF and I was keeping her.

I glanced around the yard and grinned. Mac had walked

around in shock for a few weeks as the idea of having a backyard Country Club sunk in, but he'd been a really good sport in the end. However, the ongoing game of pornographic Little Red Riding Hood and the Big Bad Wolf probably helped. I was seriously hot in my red cape.

Looking down at my feet, I grinned. Roy had made good on his promise and I was wearing the snazziest shitkickers in the land. He'd designed shoes for Sassy, Fabio, Henry, Audrey and Marge... and had a very long waiting list for the rest of the inhabitants of Assjacket.

Bermangoggleshitz was a rock star and was enjoying every moment. He'd designed ten pairs for Marge and Sassy, but that was only right. Marge was his princess and Sassy was the light of his life. I was a tiny bit jealous, but Roy had promised me that I was next in line for some insane wedges that hadn't even hit the stores yet. Cookie Witch was sporting heels today that made me salivate.

"You know you're ready," Marge said, coming up behind me and wrapping her slim arms around me.

"I have no idea what you're talking about," I said, feigning ignorance.

Marge simply laughed, kissed the top of my head and went to join her sister in the fun. She was getting as annoying as her sibling. I'd avoided my *new neighbor* like the plague. Baba Yaga was teetering on the edge of me turning her into a booby. I was not and would never be ready to take her job. I was unstable, grumpy and wildly immature.

Well... sadly less immature than I used to be.

She'd repeatedly pointed out that the last spell I'd cast to my tree buddies was profanity-free. I'd countered that by popping off a spell that had the F-bomb in it sixteen times. I'd earned a massive ass blast from the Goddess for that little ditty, but it was worth it. Baba Yaga stayed away for a week after that episode.

Roger ambled over with a sweet smile and clasped his little hands in front of him.

"I'd like to get you back on the therapy schedule," Roger said, bizarrely still sporting a kilt.

I'd repaired his pentagon of peens weeks ago, but he was clearly fond of the skirt. A few other men in town wore them as well. Fat Bastard thought it was hilarious and was now trying to get the idiots to believe man-bras were high fashion.

"That's probably a good idea," I told him. "Do you think I should get Henry and Audrey in for the sewer mouth issue?"

Roger small nose began to twitch up a storm. He stared at me and then dropped his gaze to the ground. I was aware the little bastard was trying not to laugh. It wasn't funny and I was debating if I should shrink his skirt or his underpants—if he was wearing any… Goddess, that was a bad image.

"I think we can wait on the therapy for the children. Meanwhile maybe you should invest in some duct tape," he suggested gamely and then hopped off before I could zap him bald.

As much as I wanted to chase him down, I had to admit he had a point. I loved my babies more than my own life. If I needed to seal my mouth shut, I would do it. Not happily, but I would do it.

Maturity sucked ass.

Cheesecake would help. It always helped.

Wanda, DeeDee, Jeeves and Marge had cooked up a feast for the grand opening of the Assjacket Country Club. I'd sampled everything—twice. Thank Goddess I had a metabolism faster than the speed of light.

Shifters and witches were eating, drinking and enjoying themselves. Simon and a few of the boys had set up their instruments in the gazebo that Sassy had designed and they were rocking out to the delight of the crowd. Henry, Audrey, and Wanda's little one, Bo, were dancing and laughing so hard their adorable faces were bright pink with joy. It was perfect.

"Well," Mac said, looking around, shaking his head and giving me a lopsided smile that set my panties on fire. "At least the winter is coming. We'll have to close up the pool for a while."

"Pools," I corrected him. In the end we'd left holes for two pools—an adult pool and a baby pool. Along with the fifteen hot tubs, we had a lot of holes in the back yard.

"Yes, pools," he said with a pained chuckle and then pulled me close. "How about we ditch this shindig and go play x-rated Beauty and the Beast?"

"Hold that thought," I said with a wide grin. "Incoming."

Bermangoggleshitz approached slowly, using a wooden cane graciously provided by one of my tree buddies. The warlock was doing better, but it would take time to heal from his near deathblow. I was still stunned at how gorgeous he was, but I was getting used to it. He would always be kind of a jackhole and that suited me just fine.

"So Zelda," he said with a raised brow and a hint of a smile. "I have a question for you."

"Does it have anything to do with pushups?" I asked warily. I was still training with the warlock and the asshandle had an unhealthy penchant for the exercise.

"No, it doesn't," he said with a laugh. "Describe dark magic to me."

"In words?" I asked. I loved confusing him. He was so easy.

"Umm… yes," he replied. "Words would be fine."

Without thinking, I spoke. "Rings around the sun, the Goddess's knowledge, Dragon's bones and an Angel choir." I finished.

Roy was stunned and I was as shocked as Roy. "Was that okay?" I asked.

His nod and smile of pride made me feel ten feet tall—kind of like my tree buddies. I'd named them and they'd seemed pleased —Sleepy, Doc, Sneezy, Grumpy and Sponge Bob. They had replanted themselves at the edge of my favorite hot tub, the

French. However, they were sneaky enormous freaks of nature. During the night, they would rearrange themselves, so I'd end up accidentally calling them by the wrong names every morning. They thought that was fucking hilarious. They were weird, but apparently they were mine.

Fat Bastard, Jango Fett and Boba Fett had taken to the trees immediately and were teaching them how to cheat at cards. My cats were also now doing most of their gag inducing nad cleansing rituals under the shade of Sponge Bob. As the sun moved across the sky during the day, Sponge Bob would adjust so the rotund and disgusting felines had shade.

Whatever worked. I was just happy not to have to witness the ball licking on a constant basis.

"You know what's missing?" Baba Yaga asked as she and Fabio snuck up on me from behind.

It was the only way she could talk with me as I usually ran like hell or flew away when I saw her coming.

"Sequined cone bras and feathers?" I replied.

"Always," she said with a delighted laugh. "However, that's not what I was referring to."

I waited for her to start in on me again about taking over her job, but she didn't. She had no clue how close she was edging to becoming a full body knocker—or maybe she did. She *was* the Baba Fucking Yaga.

"Fireworks," she said, clapping her well manicured hands together.

A slow smile spread across my mouth and I laughed. She was right. A few explosions would make today even better.

"Would you like to join me in making that happen?" I asked, grinning.

"Normally yes, but I have a meeting with the Goddess later and need to save my energy."

Baba Yaga had been instrumental in dealing with Endora's punishment. I was sure that was devastating to her even though

Endora had earned it. The woman was and would always be Carol's mother. I still thought about my mother from time to time, but for the most part I'd let it go. I had real tangible love in my life and I realized I didn't need hers.

I wasn't sure if it was having my own children or if learning to love myself had made me stronger, but again, I didn't put a whole lot of thought into it. Maybe Baba Yaga should have a baby… or maybe not. That led me to picture her and my father doing the nasty, which wiped the grin right off my face and made me gag. Of course then it degenerated into imagining them borrowing Roy and Marge's Twister mat and going at it in feathered cone bras under a disco ball. I was now beginning to dry heave.

"Are you okay?" Fabio asked, concerned as he pounded on my back to dislodge the cheesecake I'd shoved in to keep from screaming in horror.

"I'm good," I choked out. "Gotta go find Sassy and Marge… really need to blow some shit up."

The fireworks were cathartic and the crowd was thrilled.

"We're the Three Musketeers!" Sassy shouted with delight as we watched the sky shimmer with riotous color.

"The Three Amigos," Marge added with a laugh, sending a glittering gold, cookie-scented explosion high above our heads.

I couldn't think of anything to add that didn't have a potty word in it, so I just grinned and detonated a rainbow of a whopper into the stratosphere.

I did know this. Three was a charm. I'd gotten through the worst disaster in my life with the help of the two crazy witches beside me.

Of course, Baba Yaga had helped too. I suppose if three was a charm, four would make us fucking fantastic.

The Fantastic Fucking Four—now that was a disaster waiting to happen.

— THE END (for now) —

EXCERPT: READY TO WERE

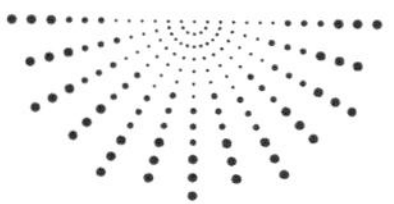

SHIFT HAPPENS, BOOK 1

CHAPTER ONE

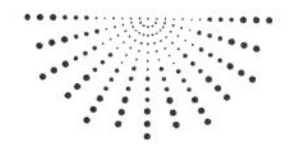

"You're joking."

"No, actually I'm not," my boss said and slapped the folder into my hands. "You leave tomorrow morning and I don't want to see your hairy ass till this is solved."

I looked wildly around her office for something to lob at her head. It occurred to me that might not be the best of ideas, but desperate times led to stupid measures. She could not do this to me. I'd worked too hard and I wasn't going back. Ever.

"First of all, my ass is not hairy except on a full moon and you're smoking crack if you think I'm going back to Georgia."

Angela crossed her arms over her ample chest and narrowed her eyes at me. "Am I your boss?" she asked.

"Is this a trick question?"

She huffed out an exasperated sigh and ran her hands through her spiked 'do making her look like she'd been electrocuted. "Essie, I am cognizant of how you feel about Hung Island, Georgia, but there's a disaster of major proportions on the horizon and I have no choice."

"Where are you sending Clark and Jones?" I demanded.

"New York and Miami."

"Oh my god," I shrieked. "Who did I screw over in a former life that those douches get to go to cool cities and I have to go home to an island called Hung?"

"Those douches *do* have hairy asses and not just on a full moon. You're the only female agent I have that looks like a model so you're going to Georgia. Period."

"Fine. I'll quit. I'll open a bakery."

Angela smiled and an icky feeling skittered down my spine. "Excellent, I'll let you tell the Council that all the money they invested in your training is going to be flushed down the toilet because you want to bake cookies."

The Council consisted of supernaturals from all sorts of species. The branch that currently had me by the metaphorical balls was WTF—Werewolf Treaty Federation. They were the worst as far as stringent rules and consequences went. The Vampyres were loosey goosey, the Witches were nuts and the freakin' Fairies were downright pushovers, but not the Weres. Nope, if you enlisted you were in for life. It had sounded so good when the insanely sexy recruiting officer had come to our local Care For Your Inner Were meeting.

Training with the best of the best. Great salary with benefits. Apartment and company car. But the kicker for me was that it was fifteen hours away from the hell I grew up in. No longer was I Essie from Hung Island, Georgia—*and who in their right mind would name an island Hung*—I was Agent Essie McGee of the Chicago WTF. The irony of the initials was a source of pain to most Werewolves, but went right over the Council's heads due to the simple fact that they were older than dirt and oblivious to pop culture.

Yes, I'd been disciplined occasionally for mouthing off to superiors and using the company credit card for shoes, but other than that I was a damn good agent. I'd graduated at the top of my class and was the go-to girl for messy and dangerous assignments that no one in their right mind would take... I'd singlehandedly brought down three rogue Weres who were selling secrets to the Dragons—another supernatural species. The Dragons shunned the Council, had their own little club and a psychotic desire to rule the world. Several times they'd come close due to the fact that they were loaded and Weres from the New Jersey Pack were easily bribed. Not to mention the fire-breathing thing...

I was an independent woman living in the Windy City. I had a gym membership, season tickets to the Cubs and a gay Vampyre best friend named Dwayne. What more did a girl need?

Well, possibly sex, but the *bastard* had ruined me for other men...

Hank "The Tank" Wilson was the main reason I'd rather chew my own paw off than go back to Hung Island, Georgia. Six foot three of obnoxious, egotistical, perfect-assed, alpha male Werewolf. As the alpha of my local Pack he had decided it was high time I got mated...to him. I, on the other hand, had plans—big ones and they didn't include being barefoot and pregnant at the beck and call of a player.

So I did what any sane, rational woman would do. I left in the middle of the night with a suitcase, a flyer from the hot recruiter and enough money for a one-way bus ticket to freedom. Of course, nothing ever turns out as planned... The apartment was the size of a shoe box, the car was used and smelled like French fries and the benefits didn't kick in till I turned one hundred and twenty five. We Werewolves had long lives.

"Angela, you really can't do this to me." Should I get down on my knees? I was so desperate I wasn't above begging.

"Why? What happened there, Essie? Were you in some kind of trouble I should know about?" Her eyes narrowed, but she wasn't yelling.

I think she liked me...kind of. The way a mother would like an annoying spastic two year old who belonged to someone else.

"No, not exactly," I hedged. "It's just that..."

"Weres are disappearing and presumed dead. Considering no

one knows of our existence besides other supernaturals, we have a problem. Furthermore, it seems like humans might be involved."

My stomach lurched and I grabbed Angela's office chair for balance. "Locals are missing?" I choked out. My grandma Bobby Sue was still there, but I'd heard from her last night. She'd harangued me about getting my belly button pierced. Why I'd put that on Instagram was beyond me. I was gonna hear about that one for the next eighty years or so.

"Not just missing—more than likely dead. Check the folder," Angela said and poured me a shot of whiskey.

With trembling hands I opened the folder. This had to be a joke. I felt ill. I'd gone to high school with Frankie Mac and Jenny Packer. Jenny was as cute as a button and was the cashier at the Piggly Wiggly. Frankie Mac had been the head cheerleader and cheated on every test since the fourth grade. Oh my god, Debbie Swink? Debbie Swink had been voted most likely to succeed and could do a double backwards flip off the high dive. She'd busted her head open countless times before she'd perfected it. Her mom was sure she'd go to the Olympics.

"I know these girls," I whispered.

"Knew. You knew them. They all were taking classes at the modeling agency."

"What modeling agency? There's no modeling agency on Hung Island." I sifted through the rest of the folder with a knot the size of a cantaloupe in my stomach. More names and faces I recognized. Sandy Moongie? *Wait a minute.*

"Um, not to speak ill of the dead, but Sandy Moongie was the size of a barn…she was modeling?"

"Worked the reception desk." Angela shook her head and dropped down on the couch.

"This doesn't seem that complicated. It's fairly black and white. Whoever is running the modeling agency is the perp."

"The modeling agency is Council sponsored."

I digested that nugget in silence for a moment.

"And the Council is running a modeling agency, why?"

"Word is that we're heading toward revealing ourselves to the humans and they're trying to find the most attractive representatives to do so."

"That's a joke, right?" *What kind of dumb ass plan was that?*

"I wish it was." Angela picked up my drink and downed it. "I'm getting too old for this shit," she muttered as she refilled the shot glass, thought better of it and just swigged from the bottle.

"Is the Council aware that I'm going in?"

"What do you think?"

"I think they're old and stupid and that they send in dispensable agents like me to clean up their shitshows," I grumbled.

"Smart girl."

"Who else knows about this? Clark? Jones?"

"They know," she said wearily. "They're checking out agencies in New York and Miami."

"Isn't it conflict of interest to send me where I know everyone?"

"It is, but you'll be able to infiltrate and get in faster that way. Besides, no one has disappeared from the other agencies yet."

There was one piece I still didn't understand. "How are humans involved?"

She sighed and her head dropped back onto her broad shoulders. "Humans are running the agency."

It took a lot to render me silent, like learning my grandma had been a stripper in her youth, and that all male Werewolves were hung like horses… but this was horrific.

"Who in the hell thought that was a good idea? My god, half the female Weres I know sprout tails when flash bulbs go off. We won't have to come out, they can just run billboards of hot girls with hairy appendages coming out of their asses."

"It's all part of the *Grand Plan*. If the humans see how wonderful and attractive we are, the issue of knowingly living alongside of us will be moot."

Again. Speechless.

"When are Council elections?" It was time to vote some of those turd knockers out.

"Essie." Angela rolled her eyes and took another swig. "There are no elections. They're appointed and serve for life."

"I knew that," I mumbled. Skipping Were History class was coming back to bite me in the butt.

"I'll go." There was no way I couldn't. Even though my knowledge of the hierarchy of my race was fuzzy, my skills were top notch and trouble seemed to find me. In any other job that would suck, but in mine, it was an asset.

"Good. You'll be working with the local Pack alpha. He's also the sheriff there. Name's Hank Wilson. You know him?"

"Yep." *Biblically. I knew the son of a bitch biblically.*

~

"YOU'RE GONNA BANG HIM."

"I am not gonna bang him."

"You are so gonna bang him."

"Dwayne, if I hear you say that I'm gonna bang him one more time, I will not let you borrow my black Mary Jane pumps. Ever again."

Dwayne made the international "zip the lip and throw away the key" sign while silently mouthing that I was going to bang Hank.

"I think you should bang him if he's a hot as you said." Dwayne made himself comfortable on my couch and turned on the TV.

"When did I ever say he was hot?" I demanded as I took the remote out of his hands. I was not watching any more *Dance Moms*. "I never said he was hot."

"Paaaaleese," Dwayne flicked his pale hand over his shoulder and rolled his eyes.

"What was that?"

"What was what?" he asked, confused.

"That shoulder thing you just did."

"Oh, I was flicking my hair over my shoulder in a *girlfriend* move."

"Okay, don't do that. It doesn't work. You're as bald as a cue ball."

"But it's the new move," he whined.

Oh my god, Vampyres were such high maintenance. "According to who?" I yanked my suitcase out from under my bed and started throwing stuff in.

"Kim Kardashian."

I refused to dignify that with so much as a look.

"Fine," he huffed. "But if you say one word about my skinny jeans I am so out of here."

I considered it, but I knew he was serious. As crazy as he drove me, I adored him. He was my only real friend in Chicago and I had no intention of losing him.

"I know he's hot," Dwayne said. "Look at you—you're so gorge it's redonkulous. You're all legs and boobs and hair and lips—you're far too beautiful to be hung up on a goober."

"Are you calling me shallow?" I snapped as I ransacked my tiny apartment for clean clothes. Damn it, tomorrow was laundry day. I was going to have to pack dirty clothes.

"So he's ugly and puny and wears bikini panties?"

"No! He's hotter than Satan's underpants and he wears boxer briefs," I shouted. "You happy?"

"He's actually a nice guy."

"You've met Hank?" I was so confused I was this close to making fun of his skinny jeans just so he would leave.

"Satan. He's not as bad as everyone thinks."

How was it that everyone I came in contact with today stole my ability to speak? Thankfully, I was interrupted by a knock at my door.

"You expecting someone?" Dwayne asked as he pilfered the remote back and found *Dance Moms*.

"No."

I peeked through the peephole. Nobody came to my place except Dwayne and the occasional pizza delivery guy or Chinese food take out guy or Indian food take out guy. *Wait. What the hell was my boss doing here?*

"Angela?"

"You going to let me in?"

"Depends."

"Open the damn door."

I did.

Angela tromped into my shoebox and made herself at home. Her hair was truly spectacular. It looked like she might have even pulled out a clump on the left side. "You want to tell me why the sheriff and alpha of Hung Island, Georgia says he won't work with you?"

"Um…no?"

"He said he had a hard time believing someone as flaky and irresponsible as you had become an agent for the Council and he wants someone else." Angela narrowed her eyes at me and took the remote form Dwayne. "Spill it, Essie."

I figured the best way to handle this was to lie—hugely. However, gay Vampyre boyfriends had a way of interrupting and screwing up all your plans.

"Well, you see…"

"He's her mate and he dipped his stick in several other… actually *many* other oil tanks. So she dumped his furry player ass, snuck away in the middle of the night and hadn't really planned on ever going back there again." Dwayne sucked in a huge breath, which was ridiculous because Vampyres didn't breathe.

It took everything I had not to scream and go all Wolfy. "Dwayne, clearly you want me to go medieval on your lily white ass because I can't imagine why you would utter such bullshit to my boss."

"Doesn't sound like bullshit to me," Angela said as she channel surfed and landed happily on an old episode of *Cagney and Lacey*. "We might have a problem here."

"Are you replacing me?" Hank Wilson had screwed me over once when I was his. He was not going to do it again when I wasn't.

"Your call," she said. Dwayne, who was an outstanding shoplifter, covertly took back the remote and flipped over to the Food Channel. Angela glanced up at the tube and gave Dwayne the evil eye.

"I refuse to watch lesbians fight crime in the eighties. I'll get hives," he explained, tilted his head to the right and gave Angela a smile. He was so pretty it was silly—piercing blue eyes and body to die for. Even my boss had a hard time resisting his charm.

"Fine," she grumbled.

"Excuse me," I yelled. "This conversation is about me, not testosterone ridden women cops with bad hair, hives or food. It's my life we're talking about here—me, me, me!" My voice had risen to decibels meant to attract stray animals within a ten-mile radius, evidenced by the wincing and ear covering.

"Essie, are you done?" Dwayne asked fearfully.

"Possibly. What did you tell him?" I asked Angela.

"I told him the Council has the last word in all matters. Always. And if he had a problem with it, he could take it up with the elders next month when they stay awake long enough to listen to the petitions of their people."

"Oh my god, that's awesome," I squealed. "What did he say?"

"That if we send you down, he'll give you bus money so you can hightail your sorry cowardly butt right back out of town."

Was she grinning at me, and was that little shit Dwayne jotting the conversation down in the notes section on his phone?

"Let me tell you something," I ground out between clenched

teeth as I confiscated Dwayne's phone and pocketed it. "I am going to Hung Island, Georgia tomorrow and I will kick his ass. I will find the killer first and then I will castrate the alpha of the Georgia Pack…with a dull butter knife."

Angela laughed and Dwayne jackknifed over on the couch in a visceral reaction to my plan. I stomped into my bathroom and slammed the door to make my point, then pressed my ear to the rickety wood to hear them talk behind my back.

"I'll bet you five hundred dollars she's gonna bang him," Dwayne told Angela.

"I'll bet you a thousand that you're right," she shot back.

"You're on."

CHAPTER TWO

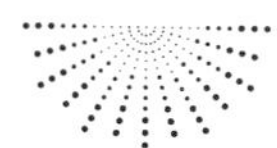

"This music is going to make me yack." Dwayne moaned and put his hands over his ears.

Trying to ignore him wasn't working. I promised myself I wouldn't put him out of the car until we were at least a hundred miles outside of Chicago. I figured anything less than that wouldn't be the kind of walk home that would teach him a lesson.

"First of all, Vampyres can't yack and I don't recall asking you to come with me," I replied and cranked up The Clash.

"You have got to be kidding." He huffed and flipped the station to Top Forty. "You need me."

"Really?"

"Oh my god," Dwayne shrieked. "I luurrve Lady Gaga."

"That's why I need you?"

"Wait. What?"

"I need you because you love The Gaga?"

Dwayne rolled his eyes. "Everyone loves The Gaga. You need me because you need to show your hometown and Hank the Hooker that you have a new man in your life."

"You're a Vampyre."

"Yes, and?"

"Well, um…you're gay."

"What does that have to do with anything? I am hotter than asphalt in August and I have a huge package."

While his points were accurate, there was no mistaking his sexual preference. The skinny jeans, starched muscle shirt, canvas Mary Janes and the gold hoop earrings were an undead giveaway.

"You know, I think you should just be my best friend. I want to show them I don't need a man to make it in this world…okay?" I glanced over and he was crying. Shitshitshit. Why did I always say the wrong thing? "Dwayne, I'm sorry. You can totally be my…"

"You really consider me your best friend?" he blubbered. "I have never had a best friend in all my three hundred years. I've tried, but I just…" He broke down and let her rip.

"Yes, you're my best friend, you idiot. Stop crying. Now." Snark I could deal with. Tears? Not so much.

"Oh my god, I just feel so happy," he gushed. "And I want you to know if you change your mind about the boyfriend thing just wink at me four times and I'll stick my tongue down your throat."

"Thanks, I'll keep that in mind."

"Anything for my best friend. Ohhh Essie, are there any gay bars in Hung?"

This was going to be a wonderful trip.

ONE WAY IN TO HUNG ISLAND, GEORGIA. ONE WAY OUT. THE BRIDGE was long and the ocean was beautiful. Sun glistened off the water and sparkled like diamonds. Dwayne was quiet for the first time in fifteen hours. As we pulled into town, my gut clenched and I started to sweat. This was stupid—so very stupid. The nostalgic pull of this place was huge and I felt sucked back in immediately.

"Holy Hell," Dwayne whispered. "It's beautiful here. How did you leave this place?"

He was right. It was beautiful. It had the small town feel mixed up with the ocean and land full of wild grasses and rolling hills. How did I leave?

"I left because I hate it here," I lied. "We'll do the job, castrate the alpha with a butter knife and get out. You got it?"

"Whatever you say, best friend. Whatever you say." He grinned.

"I'm gonna drop you off at my Grandma Bobby Sue's. She doesn't exactly know we're coming so you have to be on your best behavior."

"Will you be?"

"Will I be what?" God, Vamps were tiresome.

"On your best behavior."

"Absolutely not. We're here."

I stopped my crappy car in front of a charming old Craftsman. Flowers covered every inch of the yard. It was a literal explosion of riotous color and I loved it. Granny hated grass—found the color offensive. It was the home I grew up in. Granny BS, as everyone loved to call her, had raised me after my parents died in a horrific car accident when I was four. I barely remembered my parents, but Granny had told me beautiful bedtime stories about them my entire childhood.

"OMG, this place is so cute I could scream." Dwayne squealed and jumped out of the car into the blazing sunlight. All the stories about Vamps burning to ash or sparkling like diamonds in the sun were a myth. The only thing that could kill Weres and Vamps were silver bullets, decapitation, fire and a silver stake in the heart.

Grabbing Dwayne by the neck of his muscle shirt, I stopped him before he went tearing into the house. "Granny is old school. She thinks Vamps are…you know."

"Blood sucking leeches who should be eliminated?" Dwayne grinned from ear to ear. He loved a challenge. Crap.

"I wouldn't go that far, but she's old and set in her geezer ways. So if you have to, steer clear."

"I'll have her eating kibble out of my manicured lily white

hand in no time at…holy shit!" Dwayne screamed and ducked as a blur of Granny BS came flying out of the house and tackled my ass in a bed of posies.

"Mother Humper." I grunted and struggled as I tried to shove all ninety-five pounds of pissed off Grandma Werewolf away from me.

"Gimme that stomach," she hissed as she yanked up my shirt. Thank the Lord I was wearing a bra. Dwayne stood in mute shock and just watched me get my butt handed to me by my tiny granny, who even at eighty was the spitting image of a miniature Sophia Loren in her younger years.

"Get off of me, you crazy old bag," I ground out and tried to nail her with a solid left. She ducked and backslapped my head.

"I said no tattoos and no piercings till you're fifty," she yelled. "Where is it?"

"Oh my GOD," I screeched as I trapped her head with my legs in a scissors hold. "You need meds."

"Tried 'em. They didn't work," she grumbled as she escaped from my hold. She grabbed me from behind as I tried to make a run for my car and ripped out my belly button ring.

"Ahhhhhgrhupcraaap, that hurt, you nasty old bat from Hell." I screamed and looked down at the bloody hole that used to be really cute and sparkly. "That was a one carat diamond, you ancient witch."

Both of her eyebrows shot up and I swear to god they touched her hairline.

"Okay, fine," I muttered. "It was cubic zirconia, but it was NOT cheap."

"Hookers have belly rings," she snapped.

"No, hookers have pimps. Normal people have belly rings, or at least they used to," I shot back as I examined the wound that was already closing up.

"Come give your granny a hug," she said and put her arms out.

I approached warily just in case she needed to dole out more punishment for my piercing transgression. She folded me into her arms and hugged me hard. That was the thing about my granny. What you saw was what you got. Everyone always knew where they stood with her. She was mad and then she was done. Period.

"Lawdy, I have missed you, child," she cooed.

"Missed you too, you old cow." I grinned and hugged her back. I caught Dwayne out of the corner of my eye. He was even paler than normal if that was possible and he had placed his hands over his pierced ears.

"Granny, I brought my…"

"Gay Vampyre best friend," she finished my introduction. She marched over to him, slapped her hands on her skinny hips and stared. She was easily a foot shorter than Dwayne, but he trembled like a baby. "Do you knit?" she asked him.

"Um…no, but I've always wanted to learn," he choked out.

She looked him up and down for a loooong minute, grunted and nodded her head. "We'll get along just fine then. Get your asses inside before the neighbors call the cops."

"Why would they call the cops?" Dwayne asked, still terrified.

"Well boy, I live amongst humans and I just walloped my granddaughter on the front lawn. Most people don't think that's exactly normal."

"Point," he agreed and hightailed it to the house.

"Besides," she cackled. "Wouldn't want the sheriff coming over to arrest you now, would we?"

I rolled my eyes and flipped her the bird behind her back.

"Saw that, girlie," she said.

Holy Hell, she still had eyes in the back of her head. If I was smart, I'd grab Dwayne, get in my car and head back to Chicago… but I had a killer to catch and a whole lot to prove here. Smart wasn't on my agenda today.

CHAPTER THREE

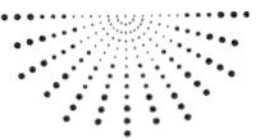

The house was exactly the same as it was the last time I saw it a year ago. Granny had more crap on her tables, walls and shelves than an antique store. Dwayne was positively speechless and that was good. Granny took her décor seriously.

"I'm a little disappointed that you want to be a model, Essie," Granny sighed. "You have brains and a mean right hook. Never thought you'd try to coast by with your looks."

I gave Dwayne the *I'll kill you if you tell her I'm an agent on a mission* look and thankfully he understood. While I hated that my granny thought I was shallow and jobless, it was far safer that she didn't know why I was really here.

"Well, you know…I just need to make a few bucks, then get back to my life in the big city," I mumbled. I was a sucky liar around my granny and she knew it.

"Hmmm," she said, staring daggers at me.

"What?" I asked, not exactly making eye contact.

"Nothin'. I'm just lookin'," she challenged.

"And what are you looking at?" I blew out an exasperated sigh and met her eyes. A challenge was a challenge and I *was* a Werewolf…

"A bald face little fibber girl," she crowed. "Spill it or I'll whoop your butt again."

Dwayne quickly backed himself into a corner and slid his phone out of his pocket. That shit was going to video my ass kicking. I had several choices here…destroy Dwayne's phone, elaborate on my lie or come clean. The only good option was the phone.

"Fine," I snapped and sucked in a huge breath. The truth will set you free or result in a trip to the ER… "I'm an agent with the Council—a trained killer for WTF and I'm good at it. The fact that I'm a magnet for trouble has finally paid off. I'm down here to find out who in the hell is killing Werewolves before it blows up in our faces. I plan to find the perps and destroy them with my own hands or a gun, whichever will be most painful. Then I'm going to castrate Hank with a dull butter knife. I plan on a short vacation when I'm done before going back to Chicago."

For the first time in my twenty-eight years on Earth, Granny was mute. It was all kinds of awesome.

"Can I come on the vacation?" Dwayne asked.

"Yes. Cat got your tongue, old woman?" I asked.

"Well, I'll be damned," she said almost inaudibly. "I suppose this shouldn't surprise me. You are a female alpha bitch."

"No," I corrected her. "I'm a lone wolf who wants nothing to do with Pack politics. Ever."

Granny sat her skinny bottom down on her plastic slipcovered floral couch and shook her head. "Ever is a long time, little girl. Well, I suppose I should tell you something now," she said gravely and worried her bottom lip.

"Oh my god, are you sick?" I gasped. Introspective thought was way out of my granny's normal behavior pattern. My stomach roiled. She was all I had left in the world and as much as I wanted to skin her alive, I loved her even more.

"Weres don't get sick. It's about your mamma and daddy. Sit down. And Dwayne, hand over your phone. If I find out you have loose lips, I'll remove them," she told my bestie.

I sat. Dwayne handed. I had thought I knew everything there was to know about my parents, but clearly I was mistaken. Hugely mistaken.

"You remember when I told you your mamma and daddy died in a car accident?"

"Yes," I replied slowly. "You showed me the newspaper articles."

"That's right." She nodded. "They did die in a car, but it wasn't no accident."

Movement was necessary or I thought I might throw up. I paced the room and tried to untangle my thoughts. It wasn't like I'd even known my parents, but they were mine and now I felt cheated somehow. I wanted to crawl out of my skin. My heart pounded so loudly in my chest I was sure the neighbors could hear it. My parents were murdered and this was the first time I was hearing about it?

"Again. Say that again." Surely I'd misunderstood. I'd always been one to jump to conclusions my entire life, but the look on Granny's face told me that this wasn't one of those times.

"They didn't own a hardware store. Well, actually I think they did, but it was just a cover."

"For what?" I asked, fairly sure I knew where this was going.

"They were WTF agents, child, and they were taken out," she said and wrapped her skinny little arms around herself. "Broke my heart—still does."

"And you never told me this? Why?" I demanded and got right up in her face.

"I don't rightly know," she said quietly. "I wanted you to grow up happy and not feel the need for revenge."

She stroked my cheek the way she did when I was a child and I leaned into her hand for comfort. I was angry, but she did what she thought was right. Needless to say, she wasn't right, but…

"Wait, why would I have felt the need for revenge?" I asked. Something was missing.

"The Council was never able to find out who did it, and after a while they gave up."

Everything about that statement was so wrong I didn't know how to react. They gave up? What the hell was that? The Council never gave up. I was trained to get to the bottom of everything. Always.

"That's the most absurd thing I've ever heard. The Council always gets their answers."

Granny shrugged her thin shoulders and rearranged the knickknacks on her coffee table. Wait. Did the Council know more about me than I did? Did my boss Angela know more of my history than I'd ever known?

"I knew that recruiter they sent down here," Granny muttered. "I told him to stay away from you. Told him the Council already took my daughter and son-in-law and they couldn't have you."

"He didn't pay me any more attention than he did anyone else," I told her.

"What did the flyer say that he gave you?"

"Same as everybody's—salary, training, benefits, car, apartment."

"Damn it to hell," she shouted. "No one else's flyer said that. I confiscated them all after the bastard left. I couldn't get to yours cause you were shacking up with the sheriff."

"You lived with Hank the Hooker?" Dwayne gasped. "I thought you just dated a little."

"Hell to the no," Granny corrected Dwayne. "She was engaged. Left the alpha of the Georgia Pack high and dry."

"Enough," I snapped. "Ancient history. I'm more concerned about what kind of cow patty I've stepped in with the Council. The *sheriff* knows why I left. Maybe the Council accepted me cause I can shoot stuff and I have no fear and they have to hire a certain quota of women and..."

"And they want to make sure you don't dig into the past," Dwayne added unhelpfully.

"You're a smart bloodsucker," Granny chimed in.

"Thank you."

"You think the Council had something to do with it," I said. This screwed with my chi almost as much as the Hank situation from a year ago. I had finally done something on my own and it might turn out I hadn't earned any of it.

"I'm not sayin' nothing like that," Granny admonished harshly. "And neither should you. You could get killed."

She was partially correct, but I was the one they sent to kill people who broke Council laws. However, speaking against the Council wasn't breaking the law. The living room had grown too small for my need to move and I prowled the rest of the house with Granny and Dwayne on my heels. I stopped short and gaped at my empty bedroom.

"Where in the hell is my furniture?"

"You moved all your stuff to Hank's and he won't give it back," Granny informed me.

An intense thrill shot through my body, but I tamped it down immediately. I was done with him and he was surely done with me. No one humiliated an alpha and got a second chance. Besides, I didn't want one... Dwayne's snicker earned him a glare that made him hide behind Granny in fear.

"Did you even try to get my stuff back?" I demanded.

"Of course I did," she huffed. "That was your mamma's set from when she was a child. I expected you'd use it for your own daughter someday."

My mamma...My beautiful mamma who'd been murdered along with my daddy. The possibility that the Council had been involved was gnawing at my insides in a bad way.

"I have to compartmentalize this for a minute or at least a

couple of weeks," I said as I stood in the middle of my empty bedroom. "I have to do what I was sent here for. But when I'm done, I'll get answers and vengeance."

"Does that mean no vacation?" Dwayne asked.

I stared at Dwayne like he'd grown three heads. He was getting terribly good at rendering me mute.

"That was a good question, Dwayne." Granny patted him on the head like a dog and he preened. "Essie, your mamma and daddy would want you to have a vacation before you get killed finding out what happened to them."

"Can we go to Jamaica?" Dwayne asked.

"Ohhh, I've never been to Jamaica," Granny volunteered.

They were both batshit crazy, but Jamaica did sound kind of nice…

"Fine, but you're paying," I told Dwayne. He was richer than Midas. He'd made outstanding investments in his three hundred years.

"Yayayayayayay!" he squealed.

"I'll call the travel agent," Granny said. "How long do you need to get the bad guy?"

"A week. Give me a week."

Want more? Visit www.robynpeterman.com.

NOTE FROM THE AUTHOR

If you enjoyed this book, please consider leaving a positive review or rating on the site where you purchased it. Reader reviews help my books continue to be valued by resellers and help new readers make decisions about reading them.

You are the reason I write these stories and I sincerely appreciate each of you!

Many thanks for your support,
~ Robyn Peterman

www.robynpeterman.com

ROBYN'S BOOK LIST

(IN CORRECT READING ORDER)

HOT DAMNED SERIES

Fashionably Dead

Fashionably Dead Down Under

Hell on Heels

Fashionably Dead in Diapers

A Fashionably Dead Christmas

Fashionably Hotter Than Hell

Fashionably Dead and Wed

Fashionably Fanged

Fashionably Flawed

A Fashionably Dead Dairy

Fashionably Forever After

SHIFT HAPPENS SERIES

Ready to Were

Some Were in Time

No Were To Run

Were Me Out

MAGIC AND MAYHEM SERIES

Switching Hour
Witch Glitch
A Witch in Time
Magically Delicious
A Tale of Two Witches
Three's A Charm

HANDCUFFS AND HAPPILY EVER AFTERS SERIES

How Hard Can it Be?
Size Matters
Cop a Feel

If after reading all the above you are still wanting more adventure and zany fun, read *Pirate Dave and His Randy Adventures*, the romance novel budding novelist Rena was helping wicked Evangeline write in *How Hard Can It Be*?
Warning: Pirate Dave Contains Romance Satire, Spoofing, and Pirates with Two Pork Swords.

ABOUT ROBYN PETERMAN

Robyn Peterman writes because the people inside her head won't leave her alone until she gives them life on paper.

Her addictions include laughing really hard with friends, shoes (the expensive kind), Target, Coke Zero Cherry with extra ice in a Styrofoam cup, bejeweled reading glasses, her kids, her super-hot hubby and collecting stray animals.

A former professional actress with Broadway, film and T.V. credits, she now lives in the South with her family and too many animals to count.

Writing gives her peace and makes her whole, plus having a job where you can work in your underpants works really well for her. You can leave Robyn a message via the Contact Page and she'll get back to you as soon as her bizarre life permits! She loves to hear from her fans!

Fun Ways To Connect With Robyn
www.robynpeterman.com
robyn@robynpeterman.com